Dangerous Connections
Vol.- IV

By

Choderlos De Laclos

Dangerous Connections
Vol.- IV
by Choderlos De Laclos

ISBN: 978-93-60468-28-6
Published by

DOUBLE 9 BOOKS

2/13-B, Ansari Road
Daryaganj, New Delhi – 110002
info@double9books.com
www.double9books.com
Tel. 011-40042856

This book is under public domain

ABOUT THE AUTHOR

Choderlos de Laclos, an 18th-century French novelist and military officer, is nice remembered for his provocative and scandalous masterpiece, "Les Liaisons Dangereuses" ("Dangerous Connections"). Born in 1741, Laclos's literary career took a prominent flip with the book of this epistolary novel in 1782. "Dangerous Connections" is a story of manipulation, seduction, and ethical decadence inside the French aristocracy. Laclos, drawing inspiration from his very own experiences within the army and the complex social milieu of pre-innovative France, weaves a narrative of intricate schemes and betrayals. The novel unfolds thru a sequence of letters exchanged amongst its characters, presenting an intimate and revealing look at their thoughts and motivations. The crucial plot revolves around the Vicomte de Valmont and the Marquise de Merteuil, foxy and amoral aristocrats who interact in a web of dangerous liaisons and sexual conquests. Laclos's narrative skillfully dissects the hypocrisy of the higher class, exposing the ethical decay below the veneer of sophistication. "Dangerous Connections" remains a conventional in French literature, celebrated for its psychological intensity, social critique, and narrative innovation. Laclos, whose lifestyles was marked through each navy and literary pursuits, left a long lasting legacy with this work, showcasing his potential to capture the complexities of human relationships and societal decadence with unprecedented finesse.

CONTENTS

LETTER CXXV
VISCOUNT DE VALMONT to the MARCHIONESS DE MERTEUIL

At last this haughty woman is conquered, who dared think she could resist me.—She is mine—totally mine.—She has nothing left to grant since yesterday.

My happiness is so great I cannot appreciate it, but am astonished at the unknown charm I feel:—Is it possible virtue can augment a woman's value even at the time of her weakness?—Avaunt such puerile ideas—don't we every day meet resistance more or less feigned at the first conquest? Yet I never experienced the charm I mean; it is not love—for although I have had fits of weakness with this amazing woman, which very much resembled that pusillanimous passion, I ever subdued them and returned to my first rules—if even the scene of yesterday should have led me farther than I intended; had I partook for a moment of the intoxication I raised, that transitory illusion would have been now evaporated, yet still the same charm remains—I own I should be pleased to indulge it, if it did not give me some uneasiness:—At my age must I then be mastered like a school-boy by an unknown and involuntary sentiment?—I must first oppose and then examine it.

Perhaps I already see into the cause—the idea pleases me—I wish it may be true.

Among the multitude of women with whom I have played the part of a lover, I never met any who were not as well inclined to surrender as I was to persuade them—I used even to call those *prudes* who met me but halfway, in contrast to so many others, whose provoking defence is intended as a cloak to their first advances.

But here I found an unfavourable prepossession against me, afterwards confirmed on the report and advice of a penetrating woman who hated me; a natural, excessive timidity, fortified with genuine modesty; a strong attachment to virtue under the powerful direction of religion, and who had already been married two years—an unsullied character—the result of those causes, which all tended to screen her from my solicitations.

It is not any way similar to my former adventures:—a mere capitulation more or less advantageous, which is easier to be acquired than to be vain of; but this is a complete victory, purchased by a hard campaign, and decided by skilful manœuvres, therefore it is not at all surprising, this success, solely my own acquisition, should be dear to me; and the increase of pleasure I experienced in my triumph, which I still feel, is no more than the soft impression of a sentiment of glory. I indulge this thought, as it saves me the humiliation of harbouring the idea of my being dependent on the very slave I have brought under subjection, as well as the disagreeable thoughts of not having within myself the plenitude of my happiness, or that the power of calling it forth into energy and making me fully enjoy it, should be revived for this or that woman exclusively of any other.

Those judicious reflections shall regulate my conduct on this important occasion and you may depend, I shall never suffer myself to be so captivated, but that I may at pleasure break those new bands:—Already I begin to talk of a rapture, and have not yet informed you how I acquired the powers—proceed and you will see to what dangers wisdom exposes itself endeavouring to assist folly—I studied my conversation and the answers to them with so much attention, I hope to be able to give you both with the utmost exactitude.

You will observe by the annexed copies of letters,[1] what kind of mediator I fixed on to gain me admittance with my fair one, with what zeal the holy man exercised himself to reunite us; I must tell you also, I learned from an intercepted letter, according to custom, the dread the humiliation of being left, had a little disconcerted the austere devotee's prudence, and stuffed her head and heart with ideas and sentiments which, though destitute of common sense, were nevertheless interesting—After these preliminaries necessary to be related, yesterday, Thursday the 28th, the day appointed by my ingrate, I presented myself as a timid and repentant slave, to retire a successful conqueror.

It was six in the evening when I came to the fair recluse; for since her return, her gates were shut against every one. She endeavoured to rise when I was announced; but her trembling knees being unable to support her, she was obliged to sit down immediately. The servant who had showed me in, having something to do in the apartment, she seemed impatient. This interval was taken up with the usual compliments. Not to lose a moment of so precious an opportunity, I examined the room carefully, and fixed my eye on the intended spot for my victory. I could have chose a more commodious one; for there was a sopha in the room: but I observed directly opposite to it a picture of the husband; and I own I was afraid with so strange a woman, a single glance, which accidentally she might cast on that side, would in an instant have destroyed a work of so much care. At last we were alone, and I entered on the business.

After relating in few words, I supposed Father Anselmus had informed her the motive of my visit, I lamented the rigorous treatment I received, and dwelt particularly on the *contempt* that had been shown. She made an apology, as I expected, and you also: but I grounded the proof on the diffidence and dread I had infused; on the scandalous flight in consequence of it, the refusal to answer my letters, or even receive them, &c. &c. As she was beginning a justification, which would have been very easy, I thought proper to interrupt her; and to compensate for this abrupt behaviour, I immediately threw in a flattery. "If such charms," said I, "have made so deep an impression on my heart, so many virtues have made as great a one on my mind. Seduced by the desire of imitating them, I had the vanity to think myself worthy of them. I do not reproach you for thinking otherwise; but I punish myself for my error." As she preserved a silent perplexity I went on. "I wish, Madam, to be justified in your sight, or obtain your pardon for all the wrongs you suppose me to have been guilty of; that I may, at least, terminate in tranquillity a life which is no longer supportable since you refuse to embellish it."

To this, however, she endeavoured to reply. "My duty would not permit me." —The difficulty to finish the fib which duty required, did not allow her to end the sentence. I replied in the most tender strain, "Is it true, then, it was me you fled from?—this retreat was necessary—and that you should put me from you—It must be so—and for ever—I should—" It is unnecessary to tell you, during this short dialogue, the tender prude's voice was oppressed, and she did not raise her eyes.

I thought it was time to animate this languishing scene; and rising in a pet,—"Your resolution, Madam," said I, "has given me back mine. We will part; and part forever: you will have leisure to congratulate yourself on your work." Surprised with this reproaching tone, she should have replied—"The resolution you have taken," said she—"Is only the effect of despair," I replied with passion. "It is your pleasure I should be miserable— you shall have the full extent of your wish. I wish you to be happy." Here the voice began to announce a strong emotion: then falling at her knees, in the dramatic style, I exclaimed, "Ah, cruel woman! Can there be happiness for me that you do not partake? How then shall I find it, when absent from you? Oh, never, never!"—I own, in abandoning myself thus, I depended much on the assistance of tears; but, whether for want of disposition, or, perhaps, only the continual, painful attention my mind was engaged in, I could not weep. Fortunately I recollected, all means are equally good to subdue a woman; and it would be sufficient to astonish her by a grand movement, to make a deep and favourable impression. I therefore made terror supply the place of absent sensibility; changing only my tone, but still preserving my posture, I continued, "Yes, at your feet I swear I will die or possess you." As I pronounced those last words our eyes met. I don't know what the timid woman saw, or thought she saw, in mine; but she rose with a terrified countenance, and escaped from my arms, which surrounded her waist: it is true, I did not attempt to hold her; for I have often observed, those scenes of despair became ridiculous when pushed with too much vivacity or lengthened out, and left no resource but what was really tragic, of which I had not the least idea. Whilst she fled from me, I added in a low disastrous tone, but so that she might hear, "Well then, death."

I rose silently, and casting a wild look on her, as if by chance, nevertheless observed her unsteady deportment, her quick respiration, her contracted muscles, her trembling, half-raised arms; every thing gave me sufficient evidence, the effect was such as I wished to produce: but as in love nothing can be brought to issue at a distance, and we were pretty far asunder, it was necessary to draw nearer. To attain which, I assumed, as soon as possible, an apparent tranquillity, proper to calm the effects of this violent agitation, without weakening the impression. My transition was:— "I am very miserable. I only wished to live for your happiness, and I have disturbed it:"—then with a composed but constrained air;—"Forgive me, Madam; little used to the rage of passions, I do not know how to suppress their violence. If I am wrong in giving way to them, I beg you will remember it shall be the last time. Compose yourself; I entreat you compose yourself." During this long discourse, I drew near insensibly. "If you wish I should be calm," replied the terrified fair, "do you then be calm." "I will then, I promise you," said I; and in a weaker tone, "If the effort is great, it ought not at least to be long: but I came to return your letters. I request you will take them. This afflicting sacrifice is the only one remaining; let me have nothing to weaken my resolution." Then drawing from my pocket the precious collection—"Here is the deceitful deposit of your friendship: it made this life supportable; take it back, and give the signal that is to separate us for ever." Here the timid lover gave way to her tender grief—"But, M. de Valmont, what is the matter? What do you mean? Is not your proceeding to-day your own voluntary act? Is it not the result of your own reflections? And is it not they have approved this necessary step, in compliance with my duty?" I replied, "Well, this step decides mine."—"And what is that?"— "The only one that can put an end to my sufferings, by parting me from you."—"But answer me what is it."—Then pressing her in my arms without any opposition, and observing from the neglect of decency, how strong and powerful her emotions were, I exclaimed, "Adorable woman! you can't conceive the love you inspire. You will never know how much you was adored, and how much dearer this passion was than my existence. May all your days be fortunate and peaceful! May they be decorated with that happiness you have deprived me of! At least, repay this sincere wish with one sigh, one tear; and be assured, the last sacrifice I make will not be the most painful to my heart. Adieu!"

Whilst I spoke, I felt her heart throb violently; her countenance altered; her tears almost suffocated her. Then I resolved to feign retreat: but she held me strongly.—"No, hear what I have to say," said she, eagerly. I answered, "Let me go."—"You shall hear me."—"I must fly from you; I must."—"No," she exclaimed; then sunk, or rather swooned in my arms. I was still doubtful of so happy an issue, seemed much terrified, and still led, or rather carried her to the place I had marked out for the field of glory. She did not recover herself until she was submitted, and given up to her happy conqueror.

So far, my lovely friend, you will perceive a methodical neatness, which I am sure will give you pleasure. You will also observe, I did not swerve in the least from the true principles of this war, which we have often remarked bore so near a resemblance to the other. Rank me, then, with the Turennes or the Fredericks. I forced the enemy to fight who was temporising. By skilful manœuvres, gained the advantage of the ground and dispositions; contrived to lull the enemy into security, to come up with him more easily in his retreat; struck him with terror before we engaged. I left nothing to chance; only a great advantage, in case of success; or a certainty of resources, in case of a defeat. Finally, the action did not begin till I had secured a retreat, by which I might cover and preserve all my former conquests. What more could be done? But I begin to fear I have enervated myself, as Hannibal did with the delights of Capua.

I expected so great an event would not pass over without the customary tears and grief. First I observed somewhat more of confusion and recollection than is usual, which I attributed to her state of prudery. Without paying much attention to those slight differences, which I imagined merely local, I followed the beaten road of consolation; fully persuaded, as commonly happens, the sensations would fly to the assistance of sentiment, that one act would prevail more than all my speeches, which I did not, however, neglect: but I met with a resistance really tremendous: less for its excess, than the form under which it appeared. Only think of a woman sitting stiff and motionless, with unalterable features; seeming divested of the faculties of thinking, hearing, or understanding, from whose eyes tears flowed without effort. Such was M. de Tourvel during my conversation. If I endeavoured to recall her attention by a caress, or even the most innocent gesture, terror immediately followed this apparent apathy, accompanied with suffocation, convulsions, sobs, and shrieks by intervals, but without a word articulated. Those fits returned several times, and always stronger; the last was even so violent, I was much frightened, and thought I had gained a fruitless victory. I returned to the usual common-place phrases—"What do you then regret you have made me the happiest man on earth?" At those words this adorable woman turned to me; her countenance, although still a little wild, had yet recovered its celestial expression. "The happiest?" said she.—You may guess my reply. "You are happy, then?"—I renewed my protestations. "Have I made you happy?"—I added praises, and every thing tender. Whilst I was speaking, all her members were stilled; she fell back softly in her chair, giving up a hand I ventured to take. "This idea relieves and consoles me," said she.

You well believe, being thus brought back in the right road, I quitted it no more; it certainly was the best, and, perhaps, the only one. When I made a second attempt, I met some resistance; what had happened before made me more circumspect: but having called on my idea of happiness for assistance, I soon experienced its favourable influence. "You are right," replied the tender creature, "I can support my existence no longer than it contributes to your happiness. I devote myself entirely to you. From this moment I give myself up to you. You shall no more experience regret or refusal from me." Thus with artless or sublime candour did she deliver her person and charms, increasing my happiness by sharing it. The intoxication was complete and reciprocal: for the first time mine survived the pleasure. I quitted her arms, only to throw myself at her feet, and swear eternal love. To own the truth, I spoke as I thought. Even after we parted, I could not shake off the idea; and I found it necessary to make extraordinary efforts to divert my attention from her.

I wish you were now here, to counterpoise the charm of the action by the reward: but I hope I shall not lose by waiting; for I look on the happy arrangement I proposed in my last letter as a settled point between us. You see I dispatch business as I promised: my affairs will be so forward, I shall be able to give you some part of my time. Quickly get rid, then, of the stupid Belleroche, and leave the whining Danceny to be engrossed solely by me. How is your time taken up in the country? You don't even answer my letters. Do you know, I have a great mind to scold you? Only prosperity is apt to make us indulgent. Besides, I can't forget ranging myself again under your banner. I must submit to your little whim. Remember, however, the new lover will not surrender any of the ancient rights of the friend.

Adieu, as formerly!—Adieu, my angel! I send you the softest kisses of love.

P. S. Poor Prevan, at the end of his month's imprisonment, was obliged to quit his corps; it is public all over Paris. Upon my word he is cruelly treated, and your success is complete.

Paris, Oct. 29, 17—.

[1] Letters cxx and cxxii.

LETTER CXXVI
MADAME DE ROSEMONDE to the
Presidente DE TOURVEL

I would have answered your letter sooner, my dear child, if the fatigue of my last had not brought on a return of my disorder, which has deprived me ever since of the use of my arm. I was very anxious to thank you for the good news you gave me of my nephew, and not less to congratulate you sincerely on your own account. Here the interposition of Providence is visible, that touching the heart of the one has also saved the other. Yes, my lovely dear! the Almighty, who sent you this trial, has assisted you in the moment your strength was exhausted; and notwithstanding your little murmurings, I think you have great reason to return him your unfeigned thanks: not but I believe you would have been very glad to have been the first in this resolution, and that Valmont's should have been the consequence of it; I even think, humanly speaking, the dignity of our sex would have been better preserved, and we are not fond of giving up any of our rights. But what are these considerations to those more important objects! We seldom hear a person saved from shipwreck complain, the means were not in his option.

You will soon experience, my dear child, the afflictions you dreaded so much will grow lighter of themselves, and even were they to last for ever in their full force, you will be sensible they are easier to bear than the remorse of guilt or self-contempt. It would have been useless to talk to you before with this apparent severity: love is an independent passion, that prudence may make us avoid, but cannot conquer, which when once it has taken root, must die its own natural death, or of absolute despair. This last being your case, gives me the resolution and the right to tell you freely my sentiments. It is cruel to frighten a sick person that is despaired of, to whom palliatives only and consolations should be administered: but it is the part of wisdom to remind those on the recovery, of the dangers they escaped, to assist them with necessary prudence and submission to the advice they stand in need of. As you have chose me for your physician, in that character I address you, and tell you, the little inconveniencies you feel at present, which may require, perhaps, some remedies, are nothing in comparison of the dreadful disorder whose cure is now certain. Then, as your friend, as the friend of a virtuous and reasonable woman, give me leave to add, this passion you have subdued, so unhappy in itself, became infinitely more so in its object. If I am to believe what I am told, my nephew, who I must own I love even to a degree of weakness, unites many laudable qualities to a great many attractions, is very dangerous to the women, blameable in his behaviour towards them, and piques himself as much on exposing as seducing them. I really believe you would have converted him. Sure never was any one so worthy; however, so many others flattered themselves in the same manner, whose hopes were frustrated, that I am overjoyed to find you are not reduced to that resource.

Reflect now, my dear woman, that instead of so many dangers as you would have had to go through, you will have, besides the testimony of a good conscience and your own peace, the satisfaction of being the cause of Valmont's reformation. I own, I think it in a great measure owing to your resolute defence, and that a moment's weakness on your part would have left my nephew in lasting disorders. I love to indulge this way of thinking, and wish you to do the same; you will find it consoling; it will be an additional reason for me to love you the more.

I shall expect you in a few days, my dear child, as you promised. You will once more find serenity and happiness where you lost them. Come and rejoice with your tender mother, that you have so happily kept your word to do nothing unworthy yourself or her.

Castle of — —, Oct. 30, 17—.

LETTER CXXVII
The MARCHIONESS DE MERTEUIL
to the VISCOUNT DE VALMONT

It was not for want of time, that I did not answer your letter of the 19th, Viscount, but plainly because it put me out of temper, and did not contain a single syllable of common sense. I thought it then the best way to leave it in oblivion—but since you seem fond of this production, and the sublime ideas it contains, that you construe my silence into consent, it is necessary you should have my opinion explicitly.

I may have heretofore formed the design of singly performing the functions of a whole seraglio; but it never entered my head to become only a part of one; this I thought you knew, now, that you cannot plead ignorance, you may readily conceive how ridiculous your proposition must appear to me. Should I sacrifice an inclination, and a new one, for you? And in what manner, pray? Why, waiting for my turn, like a submissive slave, the sublime favours of your *highness*. When, for example, you was inclined to relax for a moment from *that unknown charm* that the *adorable, the celestial* M. de Tourvel only had made you feel;—or when you dread to risk with the *engaging Cecilia*, the superior idea you wished her to preserve for you;—then condescending to stoop to me, you will seek pleasures less violent, but of not much consequence, and your inestimable bounty, though scarce, must fill the measure of my felicity. Certainly you stand high in your own opinion; and my modesty nor my glass have yet prevailed on me to think I am sunk so low. This may be owing to my wrong way of thinking; but I beg you will be persuaded I have more imaginations of the same kind.

One especially, which is, that *Danceny, the school-boy, the whiner*, totally taken up with me, sacrificing, without making a merit of it, his first love, even before it was enjoyed, and loving me to that excess that is usual with those at his age, may contribute more to my happiness and pleasure than you—I will even take the liberty to add, that if I had the inclination to give him a partner, it should not be you, at least now.

Perhaps you'll ask me why? Probably I should be at a loss for a reason; for the same whim that would give you the preference, might also exclude you. However, politeness requires I should inform you of my motive—I think you must make too many sacrifices; and instead of being grateful, as you certainly would expect, I should be inclined to think you still owed me more—You must therefore be sensible, our manner of thinking being so opposite, we can by no means unite: I fear it will be some time, nay a great while, before I change my opinion.

When that happens, I promise to give you notice:—Until then, let me advise you to take some other measures, and keep your kisses for those to whom they will be more agreeable.

You say *adieu, as formerly!* but formerly, if I remember, you set a greater value on me than to appoint me entirely to the third characters; and was content to wait until I answered in the affirmative, before you was certain of my consent: don't be angry then, if instead of saying adieu, as formerly, I say adieu, as at present.

Your servant, Viscount.

The castle of — —, Oct. 31, 17—.

LETTER CXXVIII
The Presidente DE TOURVEL to MADAME DE ROSEMONDE

I did not receive, until yesterday, Madam, your dilatory answer—it would instantly have put an end to my existence if I had any left; but M. de Valmont is now in possession of it: you see I do not conceal any thing from you; if you no longer think me worthy your friendship, I dread the loss of it less than to impose on you; to tell you all in all, I was placed by M. de Valmont, between his death and happiness—I chose the latter—I neither boast nor accuse myself; I relate the fact plainly as it is.

You will readily perceive, after this, what kind of impression your letter, and the truths it contains, must have made on me. Do not, however, imagine, it could give birth to any repining, or ever make me alter my sentiments or conduct; not that I am exempt from some torturing moments; but when my heart is rent, and I dread not being any longer able to bear my torments, I say to myself, Valmont is happy; and at this idea my miseries vanish; all is converted into joy.

It is to your nephew, then, I have devoted myself; it is for his sake I am undone; he is now the centre of my thoughts, sentiments, and actions. Whilst my life can contribute to his happiness, I shall cherish it; I shall think it fortunate; if he should hereafter think otherwise, he shall never hear from me either complaint or reproach. I have already ventured to fix my eyes on this fatal period, and my resolution is taken.

You will now perceive how little I am affected with the dread you seem to entertain, that M. de Valmont, will one day or other defame me—Before that happens, he must lose the affection he has for me; that once lost, of what signification will vain reproaches be which I shall never hear? He alone will judge me, as I will have lived for him, and him only; and my memory will repose in him; and if he will be obliged to acknowledge I loved him, I shall be justified sufficiently.

Now, Madam, you read my heart—I preferred the misfortune of being deprived of your esteem by my candour, to that of making myself unworthy of it by the baseness of a lie. I thought I owed this entire confidence to your former goodness; the addition of a word would, perhaps, give room to suspect I should be vain enough yet to depend on it; far from it: I will do myself justice, by giving up all pretensions to it.

I am with great respect, Madam, your most humble and most obedient servant.

Paris, Nov. 1, 17—.

LETTER CXXIX
VISCOUNT DE VALMONT to the MARCHIONESS DE MERTEUIL

Whence arises, my charming friend, this strain of acrimony and ridicule which runs through your last letter? What crime have I unintentionally committed which puts you so much out of temper? You reproach me with presuming on your consent before I had obtained it—I imagined, however, what might appear like presumption in any one else, would, between you and me, be only the effect of confidence. I would be glad to know how long has this sentiment been detrimental to friendship or love? Uniting hope with desire, I only complied with that natural impulse, which makes us wish to draw as near as possible to the happiness we are in pursuit of—and you have mistaken that for vanity, which is nothing more than ardour. I know very well, in such cases, custom has introduced a respectful apprehension; but you also know, it is only a kind of form, a mere precedent; and I imagined myself authorised to believe those trifling niceties no longer necessary between us.

I even think this free and open method much preferable to insipid flattery, which so often love nauseates, when it is grounded on an old connection. Moreover, perhaps the preference I give this method proceeds from the happiness it recalls to my memory—this gives me more uneasiness that you should take it in another light. However, this is the only thing that I am culpable in—for I cannot believe you can seriously imagine, that the woman exists who I would prefer to you; and still less, that I should estimate you so little as you feign to believe. You say, you have consulted your glass on this occasion, and you do not find yourself sunk so low—I believe it; and that only proves your glass to be true—but should you not rather from thence concluded that certainly that was not my opinion.

In vain I seek the cause of this strange idea—however, I suspect it is more or less dependent on the praises I lavished on other women—at least, this I infer, from the affectation of quoting the epithets, *adorable, celestial, attaching*, which I used, speaking of Madam de Tourvel, and the little Volanges: but you are not to be told, those words, which are oftener the effect of chance than reflection, express more the situation one happens to be in at the time, than the value one sets upon the person. If at the time I was affected with the one or the other, I nevertheless rapturously wished for you—If I gave you an eminent preference over both, as I would not renew our first connection without breaking off the two others, I do not think there is such great reason for reproaches.

I shall not find it more difficult to exculpate myself from the charge of the *unknown charm*, which, it seems, shocks you not a little; for being unknown, it does not follow that it is stronger—What can equal the delights you alone can always embellish with novelty and bliss? I only wished to convey to you an idea, it was a kind I never before experienced; but without pretending to give it any rank; and added, what I again repeat, whatever it be, I will overcome it: and shall exert myself more zealously if I can in this trifling affair, to have one homage more to offer to you.

As to the little Cecilia, it is useless to mention her: you have not forgot it was at your instance I took charge of this child; and only wait your orders to be rid of her. I may have made some remarks on her bloom and innocence; and for a moment thought her *engaging*, because one is always more or less pleased with their work; but she has not, in any shape, consistency to fix the attention.

Now, my lovely friend, I appeal to your justice, your first attachment to me, the long and sincere friendship, the unbounded confidence which have linked us together—have I deserved the severe manner in which you have treated me? But how easy can you make me amends when you please! Speak but the word, and you will see whether all the charms, all the attachments will keep me here, not a day, but even a minute; I will fly to your feet—into your arms—and will prove a thousand times, and in a thousand ways, that you are, you ever will be, the only mistress of my heart.

Adieu, my lovely friend! I wait your answer impatiently.

Paris, Nov. 3, 17—.

LETTER CXXX
MADAME DE ROSEMONDE, to
the Presidente DE TOURVEL

Why, my lovely dear, will you no longer be my daughter? Why do you seem to announce that our correspondence is to cease?[1] Is it to punish me for not guessing at what was improbable; or do you suspect me of creating you affliction designedly? I know your heart too well, to imagine you would entertain such an opinion of mine.—The distress your letter plunges me in is much less on my own account than yours. Oh! my young friend, with grief I tell you, you are too worthy of being beloved ever to be happy in love—Where is there a truly delicate and sensible woman, who has not met unhappiness where she expected bliss? Do men know how to rate the women they possess?

Not but many of them are virtuous in their addresses and constant in their affections—but even among those, how few that know how to put themselves in unison with our hearts. I do not imagine, my dear child, their affection is like ours—They experience the same transport often with more violence, but they are strangers to that uneasy officiousness, that delicate solicitude, that produces in us those continual tender cares, whose sole aim is the beloved object—Man enjoys the happiness he feels, woman that she gives.

This difference, so essential, and so seldom observed, influences in a very sensible manner, the totality of their respective conduct. The pleasure of the one is to gratify desires; but that of the other is to create them. To know to please, is in man the means of success; and in woman it is success itself.

And do not imagine, the exceptions, be they more or less numerous, that may be quoted, can be successfully opposed to those general truths, which the voice of the public has guaranteed, with the only distinction as to men of infidelity from inconstancy; a distinction of which they avail themselves, and of which they should be ashamed; which never has been adopted by any of our sex but those of abandoned characters, who are a scandal to us, and to whom all methods are acceptable which they think may deliver them from the painful sensation of their own meanness.

I thought, my lovely dear, those reflections might be of use to you, in order to oppose the chimerical ideas of perfect happiness, with which love never fails to amuse our imagination. Deceitful hope! to which we are still attached, even when we find ourselves under the necessity of abandoning it—whose loss multiplies and irritates our already too real sorrows, inseparable from an ardent passion—This task of alleviating your troubles, or diminishing their number, is the only one I will or can now fulfil—In disorders which are without remedy, no other advice can be given, than as to the regimen to be observed—The only thing I wish you to remember is, that to pity is not to blame a patient. Alas! who are we, that we dare blame one another? Let us leave the right of judging to the searcher of hearts; and I will even venture to believe, that in his paternal sight, a crowd of virtues, may compensate a single weakness.

But I conjure you above all things, my dear friend, to guard against violent resolutions, which are less the effects of fortitude than despondency: do not forget, that although you have made another possessor of your existence (to use your own expression) you had it not in your power to deprive your friends of the share they were before possessed of, and which they will always claim.

Adieu, my dear child! Think sometimes on your tender mother; and be assured you always will be, above every thing, the dearest object of her thoughts.

Castle of — —, Nov. 4, 17—.

[1] See Letter cxxviii.

LETTER CXXXI
The MARCHIONESS DE MERTEUIL
to the VISCOUNT DE VALMONT

Very well, Viscount; come, I am better pleased with you than I was before: now let us converse in a friendly manner, and I hope to convince you, the scheme you propose would be the highest act of folly in us both.

Have you never observed that pleasure, which is the *primum mobile* of the union of the sexes, is not sufficient to form a connection between them? and that if desire, which brings them together, precedes it, it is nevertheless followed by disgust, which repels it—This is a law of nature, that love alone can alter; and pray, can we have this same love at will? It is then necessary it should be always ready, which would have been very troublesome had it not been discovered, it is sufficient if it exists on one side: by this means the difficulty is lessened by half, even without apparent prejudice; for the one enjoys the happiness of loving, the other of pleasing—not perhaps in altogether so lively a manner, but that is compensated by deceit, which makes the balance, and then all is right.

But say, Viscount, which of us two will undertake to deceive the other? You know the story of the two sharpers who discovered each other at play— "We must not prejudice ourselves," said they; "let us club for the cards, and leave off." Let us follow this prudent advice, nor lose time together, which we may so usefully employ elsewhere.

To convince you that I consult your interest as much as my own, and that I am not actuated either by ill humour or capriciousness, I will not refuse your reward—I am very sensible one night will be sufficient; and do not in the least doubt, we shall know how to make it so pleasing, the morning will come with regret—but let us not forget, this regret is necessary to happiness; although the illusion may be enchanting, nor flatter ourselves it can be durable.

You see I fulfil my promise in my turn, and even before you perform the conditions stipulated—for I was to have had your celestial prude's first letter. Whether you do not choose to part with it, or that you have forgot the conditions of a bargain that is not so interesting to you as you would have me think, I have not received any thing; and I am much mistaken, or the tender devotee must have wrote a great deal; for how can she employ her time alone? she certainly has not sense enough for dissipation? If I was inclined, then, I have room to make you some little reproaches, which I shall pass over in silence, in consideration of the petulance I perhaps showed in my last letter.

Nothing more remains, now, Viscount, but to make you a request, and it is as much for you as myself; that is, to defer the time, which perhaps I wish for as much as you, but which I think may be put off until my return to town. On the one hand, it would be very inconvenient here; and on the other, it would be running too great a risk; for a little jealousy would fix me with the dismal Belleroche, who no longer holds but by a thread. He is already struggling to love me; we are at present so critically circumstanced, I blend as much malice as prudence in the caresses I lavish on him; at the same time you will observe, it would not be a sacrifice worthy of you—A reciprocal infidelity will add power to the charm.

Do you know I regret sometimes we are reduced to those resources—At the time we loved each other, for I believe it was love, I was happy—and you, Viscount—but why engage our thoughts on a happiness that can never return? No, say what you will, it is impossible—First, I should require sacrifices that you could not or would not make; that probably I do not deserve. Again, how is it possible to fix you? Oh, no; I will not even think of it; and notwithstanding the pleasure I now have in writing to you, I prefer quitting you abruptly. Adieu, Viscount.

Castle of — —, Nov. 6, 17—.

LETTER CXXXII
The Presidente DE TOURVEL to MADAME DE ROSEMONDE

Deeply impressed, Madam, with your goodness, to which I would entirely abandon myself, if I was not restrained from accepting by the dread of profaning it. Why, convinced of its inestimable value, must I know myself no longer worthy of it? Let me, at least, attempt to testify my gratitude. I shall admire, above all, the lenity of virtue, which views weakness with the eye of compassion; whose powerful charm preserves its forcible but mild authority over hearts, even by the side of the charm of love.

Can I still be worthy a friendship, which is no longer useful to my happiness? I must say the same of your advice. I feel its force, but cannot follow it. How is it possible to discredit perfect happiness, when I experience it this moment? If men are such as you describe them, they must be shunned, they are hateful: but where is the resemblance between Valmont and them? If, in common with them, he has that violence of passion you call transport, is it not restrained by delicacy? My dear friend, you talk of sharing my troubles; take a part, then, in my happiness; to love I am indebted for it, and how immensely does the object raise its value! You love your nephew, you say, perhaps, with fondness: ah! if you knew him as I do, you would idolize him, and yet even less than he deserves. He has undoubtedly been led astray by some errors; he does not conceal it; but who like him ever knew what was love? What can I say more? He feels it as he inspires it. You will think this is *one of the chimerical ideas with which love never fails to abuse our imagination:* but in my case, why should he be more tender, more earnest, when he has nothing farther to obtain? I will own, I formerly thought I observed an air of reflection and reserve, which seldom left him, and which often, contrary to my inclination, recalled to me the false and cruel impressions that were given me of him; but since he has abandoned himself without constraint to the emotions of his heart, he seems to guess at all my desires. Who knows but we were born for each other? If this happiness was not reserved for me to be necessary to his!—Ah! if it be an illusion, let me die before it ends.—No, I must live to cherish, to adore him. Why should he cease loving me? What woman on earth could he make happier than me? And I experience it by myself, this happiness that he has given rise to, is the only and the strongest tie. It is this delicious sentiment that exalts and purifies love, and becomes truly worthy a tender and generous mind, such as Valmont's.

Adieu, my dear, my respectable, my indulgent friend! Vainly should I think of continuing my letter. This is the hour he promised to come, and every idea flies before him. Your pardon. But you wish me happiness; it is now so great I can scarce support it.

Paris, Nov. 7, 17—.

LETTER CXXXIII
The VISCOUNT DE VALMONT to the MARCHIONESS DE MERTEUIL

What, then, my charming friend, are those sacrifices you think I would not make to your pleasure? Let me only know them; and if I hesitate to offer them to you, I give you leave to refuse the homage. What opinion have you of late conceived of me, when even favourably inclined, you doubt my sentiments or inclinations? Sacrifices that I would not or could not make! So you think I am in love, subdued! The value I set on the success, you suspect is attached to the person. Ah! thank heaven, I am not yet reduced to that, and I offer to prove it. I will prove it, if even it should be at Madame de Tourvel's expence. Certainly after that you cannot have a doubt remaining.

I may, I believe, without committing myself, give up some time to a woman, who, at least, has the merit of being of a cast rarely met. The dead season, perhaps, when this adventure took its rise, was another reason to give myself totally up to it; even now that the grand current of company scarcely begins to flow, it is not surprising my time is almost entirely taken up with her. I beg you will also recollect, it is scarce eight days I enjoy the fruits of three months labour. I have often indulged longer with what has not been so valuable, and had not cost me so much; and yet you never from thence drew any conclusions against me.

Shall I tell you the real cause of my assiduity? It is this. She is naturally of a timid disposition; at first she doubted incessantly of her happiness, which was sufficient to disturb it; so that I but just begin to observe how far my power extends in this kind. This I was curious to know, and the occasions are not so readily offered as one may think.

In the first place, pleasure is nothing but mere pleasure with a great number of women, and never any thing else; with them, whatever titles they think proper to adorn us with, we are never but factors, simple commissioners, whose activity is all their merit, and among whom he who performs most is always esteemed the best.

In another class, the most numerous now-a-days, the celebrity of the lover, the pleasure of carrying him from a rival, the dread of a reprisal again, totally engage the women. Thus we are concerned more or less in this kind of happiness which they enjoy; but it depends more on circumstances than on the person: it comes to them by us, and not from us.

It was then necessary to find a woman of delicacy and sensation to make my observations on, whose sole concern should be love, and in that passion be absorbed by the lover; whose emotions, disdaining the common track, should fly from the heart to the senses; who I have viewed, (I don't mean the first day) rise from the bed of delight all in tears, and the instant after recover voluptuousness by a word that touched her soul. She must also have united that natural candour, which habitude had made insurmountable, and would not suffer her to dissemble the least sentiment of her heart. You must agree with me, such women are scarce; and I am confident, if I had not met this one, I never should have found another.

Therefore it is not at all surprising she should have fascinated me longer than another; and if the time I spend makes her happy, perfectly happy, why should I refuse it, especially when it is so agreeable to me? But because the mind is engaged, must the heart be enslaved? Certainly not. And the value I set on this adventure will not prevent my engaging in others, or even sacrificing this to some more agreeable one.

I am even so much at liberty, that I have not neglected the little Volanges, to whom I am so little attached. Her mother brings her to town in three days, and I have secured my communication since yesterday; a little money to the porter, a few soft speeches to the waiting maid, did the business. Would you believe it? Danceny never thought of this simple method. Where, then, is the boasted ingenuity of love? Quite the contrary; it stupifies its votaries. Shall I not, then, know how to preserve myself from it? Be not uneasy, in a few days I shall divide the impression, perhaps rather too strong, it made on me, and weaken it; if one will not do, I will increase them.

Nevertheless, I shall be ready to give up the young pensioner to her discreet lover, when you think proper. I can't see you have any longer reason to oppose it. I freely consent to render poor Danceny this signal service: upon my word, it is but trifling, for all those he has done for me. He is now in the greatest anxiety to know whether he will be admitted at Madame de Volanges's. I keep him as easy as possible, by promising some how or other to gratify him one of those days; in the mean time, I take upon me to carry on the correspondence, which he intends to resume on his Cecilia's arrival. I have already six of his letters, and shall have one or two more before the happy day. This lad must have very little to do.

However, let us leave this childish couple, and come to our own business, that I may be entirely engaged with the pleasing hope your letter has given me. Do you doubt of fixing me yours? If you do, I shall not forgive you. Have I ever been inconstant? Our bands have been loosened, but never broken; our pretended rupture was an error only of the imagination; our sentiments, our interests, are still the same. Like the traveller who returned undeceived, I found out, as he did, I quitted happiness to run after hope. [1] The more strange lands I saw, the more I I loved my country. No longer oppose the idea, or sentiment rather, that brings you back to me. After having tried all manner of pleasures in our different excursions, let us sit down and enjoy the happiness of knowing, that none is equal to what we have experienced, and that we shall again find more delicious.

Adieu, my lovely friend! I consent to wait your return; however, hasten it as much as possible, and do not forget how much I wish for it.

Paris, Nov. 8, 17—.

[1] Du Belloi's tragedy of the Siege of Calais.

LETTER CXXXIV
MARCHIONESS DE MERTEUIL to
the VISCOUNT DE VALMONT

Upon my word, Viscount, you are exactly like the children, before whom one cannot speak a word, nor show a thing but they must have it immediately. Because I just mention an idea that came into my head, which I even told you I was not fixed on, you abuse my intention, and want to tie me down, at the time I endeavour to forget it, and force me in a manner to share your thoughtless desires. Are you not very ungenerous to make me bear the whole burthen of prudential care? I must again repeat, and it frequently occurs to me, the method you propose is impossible. When you would even throw in all the generosity you mention, do you imagine I am divested of my delicacies, and I would accept sacrifices prejudicial to your happiness?

My dear Viscount, you certainly deceive yourself in the sentiment that attaches you to M. de Tourvel. It is love, or such a passion never had existence. You deny it in a hundred shapes; but you prove it in a thousand. What means, for example, the subterfuge you use against yourself, for I believe you sincere with me, that makes you relate so circumstantially the desire you can neither conceal nor combat, of keeping this woman? Would not one imagine, you never had made any other happy, perfectly happy? Ah! if you doubt it, your memory is very bad: but that is not the case. To speak plainly, your heart imposes on your understanding, and pays it off with bad arguments: but I, who am so strongly interested not to be deceived, am not so easily blinded.

Thus, as I remarked, your politeness made you carefully suppress every word you thought would displease me, I could not help observing, perhaps, without taking notice of it; nevertheless you preserved the same ideas. It is no longer the adorable, the celestial Madame de Tourvel, but *an astonishing woman, a delicate sentimental woman,* even to the exclusion of all others; *a wonderful woman, such as a second could not be found.* The same way with your unknown charm, which is not *the strongest.* Well; be it so: but since you never found it out till then, it is much to be apprehended you will never meet it again; the loss would be irreparable. Those, Viscount, are sure symptoms of love, or we must renounce the hope of ever finding it. You may be assured I am not out of temper now; and have made a promise, I will not be so any more: I foresee it might become a dangerous snare. Take my word for it, we had better remain as we are, in friendship. Be thankful for my resolution in defending myself; for sometimes one must have it, not to take a step that may be attended with bad consequences.

It is only to persuade you to be of my opinion, I answer the demand you make, on the sacrifices I would exact, and you could not make. I designedly use the word exact, because immediately you will think me too exacting—so much the better: far from being angry with your refusal, I shall thank you for it. Observe, I will not dissemble with you; perhaps I have occasion for it.

First I would exact—take notice of the cruelty! that this same rare, this astonishing Madame de Tourvel, should be no more to you than any other woman; that is, a mere woman: for you must not deceive yourself; this charm, that you believe is found in others, exists in us, and it is love only embellishes the beloved object so much. What I now require, although so impossible for you to grant, you would not hesitate to promise, nay, even to swear; but I own I would not believe you the more. I could not be convinced, but by the whole tenor of your conduct.

That is not all; I should be whimsical, perhaps; the sacrifice you so politely offer me of the little Cecilia, does not give me the least uneasiness: on the contrary, I should require you to continue this toilsome duty until farther orders. Whether I should like thus to abuse my power, or whether more indulgent, or more reasonable, it would satisfy me to dispose of your sentiments without thwarting your pleasures. I would, however, be obeyed, and my commands would be very severe.

Certainly I should think myself obliged to thank you, and, who knows? perhaps to reward you. As for instance, I might shorten an absence, which would be insupportable to me. I should at length see you again, Viscount; and see you again—How?—Remember this is only a conversation, a plain narrative of an impossible scheme. I must not be the only one to forget it.

I must tell you my lawsuit begins to make me a little uneasy. I was determined to know exactly what my pretensions were. My lawyers have quoted me some laws, and a great many *authorities*, as they call them; but I can't perceive so much reason and justice in them. I am almost afraid I did wrong to refuse the compromise; however, I begin to be encouraged, when I consider my attorney is skilful, my lawyer eloquent, and the plaintiff handsome. If those reasons were to be no longer valid, the course of business must be altered; then what would become of the respect for old customs? This lawsuit is actually the only thing keeps me here. That of Belleroche is finished; the indictment quashed, each party to bear their own costs: he even is regretting not to be at the ball to-night; the regret of a man out of employment. I shall let him free at my return to town. In making this grievous sacrifice, I am consoled by the generosity he finds in it.

Adieu, Viscount! write to me often. The particulars of your amusements will make me amends partly for the dulness I suffer.

Castle of — —, Nov. 11, 17—.

LETTER CXXXV
The Presidente DE TOURVEL to MADAME DE ROSEMONDE

I am now endeavouring to write to you, and know not whether I shall be able. Gracious God!—excessive happiness prevented my continuing my last letter; now despair overwhelms me, and leaves me only strength sufficient to tell my sorrows, and deprives me of the power of expressing them.—Valmont—Valmont no longer loves me! He never loved me! Love does not depart thus. He deceived me, he betrayed me, he insults me! I suffer every kind of misfortune and humiliation; and all proceed from him.

Do not think it a mere suspicion. I was far from having any. I have not even the consolation of a doubt: I saw it. What can he say in his justification?— But what matters it to him? He will not attempt it even.—Unhappy wretch! What avail thy reproaches and thy tears? He is not concerned about thee.

It is, then, too true, he has made me a sacrifice; he has even exposed me—and to whom?—To a vile creature.—But what do I say? Ah! I have no right to despise her. She has not broke through any ties; she is not so culpable as I am. Oh! what grief can equal that which is followed by remorse! I feel my torments increase. Adieu, my dear friend! though I am unworthy your compassion, still you will have some left for me, if you can form an idea of my sufferings.

I have just read over my letter, and perceive it gives you no information. I will endeavour to muster up resolution to relate this cruel event. It was yesterday, I was to sup abroad for the first time since my return. Valmont came to me at five; he never appeared so endearing: he did not seem pleased with my intention of going abroad; I immediately resolved to stay at home. In two hours after, his air and tone changed visibly on a sudden. I don't know any thing escaped me to displease him; however, he pretended to recollect business that obliged him to leave me, and went away; not without expressing a tender concern, which I then thought very sincere.

Being left alone, I resolved to fulfil my first engagement, as I was at liberty. I finished my toilet, and got in my carriage. Unfortunately my coachman drove by the opera, and my carriage was stopped in the crowd coming up. I perceived at a little distance before mine, and the range next to me, Valmont's carriage: my heart instantly palpitated, but not with fear; and my only wish was, that my carriage should get forward: instead of which, his was obliged to back close to mine. I immediately looked out; but what was my astonishment to see beside him a well-known courtezan! I drew back, as you may believe; I had seen enough to wound my heart: but what you will scarcely credit is, this same girl, being probably in his confidence, did not turn her eyes from me, and with repeated peals of laughter stared me out of countenance.

Notwithstanding my abject state, I suffered myself to be carried to the house where I was to sup. I found it impossible to stay there long; every instant I was ready to faint, and could not refrain from tears.

At my return I wrote to M. de Valmont, and sent my letter immediately; he was not at home. Being determined at all events to be relieved from this miserable state, or have it confirmed for ever, I sent the servant back, with orders to wait: before twelve he came home, telling me the coachman was returned, and had informed him, his master would not be home for the night. This morning I thought it would be better to request he would give up my letters, and beg of him never to see me more. I have given orders accordingly, but certainly they were useless. It is now near twelve; he has not yet appeared, nor have I received a line from him.

Now, my dear friend, I have nothing farther to add. You are informed of every thing, and you know my heart. My only hope is, I shall not long trouble your tender friendship.

Paris, Nov. 15, 17—.

LETTER CXXXVI
The Presidente DE TOURVEL to the VISCOUNT DE VALMONT

Certainly, Sir, after what passed yesterday, you do not expect I should see you again, and you as certainly do not desire it. The intention of this note, then, is not so much to require you never to come near me more, as to call on you for my letters, which ought not to have existed. If they could at any time have been interesting, as proofs of the infatuation you had occasioned, they must be, now that is dissipated, indifferent to you, as they were only proofs of a sentiment you have destroyed.

I own, I was very wrong in placing a confidence in you, of which so many before me have been victims; I accuse no one but myself: but I never thought I deserved to be exposed by you to contempt and insult. I imagined, that making a sacrifice of every thing, and giving up for you my pretensions to the esteem of others, as also my own, I might have expected not to be treated by you with more severity than by the public, whose opinion always makes an immense difference between the weak and the depraved. Those are the only wrongs I shall mention. I shall be silent on those of love, as your heart would not understand mine. Farewell, Sir!

Paris, Nov. 15, 17—.

LETTER CXXXVII
VISCOUNT DE VALMONT to the
Presidente DE TOURVEL

This instant only have I received your letter, Madam. I could not read it without shuddering, and have scarcely strength to answer it. What a horrible opinion have you, then, conceived of me! Doubtless, I have my faults, and such as I shall never forgive myself, if even you should hide them with your indulgence. But how distant from my thoughts are those you reproach me! Who, me insult you! Me make you contemptible, at a time when I reverence as much as cherish you! when you raised my vanity by thinking me worthy of you! Appearances have deceived you. I will not deny they make against me: but had you not sufficient within your own heart to contend against them? Did it not revolt at the idea of having a cause of complaint against me? Yet you believed it! Thus you not only thought me capable of this atrocious frenzy, but even dreaded you had exposed yourself to it by your indulgence. Ah! if you think yourself so much degraded by your love, I must be very despicable in your sight. Oppressed by the painful sense of this idea, I lose the time I should employ in destroying it, endeavouring to repel it. I will confess all: another consideration still prevents me. Must I go back to facts I would wish to forget for ever, and recall your attention and my own to errors I shall ever repent; the cause of which I cannot yet conceive, which fill me with mortification and despair. If I excite your anger by accusing myself, the means of revenge will not be out of your reach; it will be sufficient to abandon me to my own remorse.

Yet the first cause of this unhappy event is, the all-powerful charm I feel in being with you: it was it made me too long forget an important business that could not be put off. I stayed with you so long, I did not find the person at home I wanted to see; I expected to have met her at the opera, where I was also disappointed. Emily, who I met there, and knew at a time when I was a stranger to you and love, Emily had not her carriage, and requested I would set her down at a little distance from thence; I consented, as a matter of no consequence. It was then I met you. I was instantly seized with the apprehension you would think me guilty.

The dread of afflicting or displeasing you is so powerful, it is impossible for me to conceal it, and was soon perceived. I will even own, it induced me to prevail on this girl not to show herself; this precaution, the result of delicacy, was unfavourable to love: but she, like the rest of her tribe, accustomed to the abuse of her usurped power, would not let slip so splendid an opportunity. The more she observed my embarrassment increase, the more she affected to show herself; and her ridiculous mirth, which I blush to think you could for a moment imagine yourself to be the object, had no other foundation than the cruel anxiety I felt, which proceeded from my love and respect.

So far, doubtless, I am more unfortunate than guilty. Those crimes being thus done away, I am clear of reproach. In vain, however, are you silent on those of love, which I must break through, as it concerns me so much.

Not but, in my confusion for this unaccountable misconduct, which I cannot without great grief recall to my remembrance; yet I am so sensible of my error, I would patiently bear the punishment, wait my pardon from time, from my excessive love, and my repentance; only what I yet have to say concerns your delicacy.

Do not think I seek a pretence to excuse or palliate my fault; I confess my guilt: but I do not acknowledge, nor ever will, this humiliating error can be a crime of love. For where is the analogy between a surprise of the sensations, a moment of inadvertency, which is soon replaced by shame and regret, and an immaculate sentiment, which delicate souls are only capable of, supported by esteem, and of which happiness is the fruit? Ah! do not thus profane love; or, rather, do not profane yourself, by uniting in the same point of view what never can be blended. Leave to despicable and degraded women the dread of a rivalship, and experience the torments of a cruel and humiliating jealousy; but turn your eyes from objects that would sully them: and pure as the Divinity, punish the offence without feeling it.

What punishment can you inflict on me will be more sorrowful than what I already feel—that can be comparable to the grief of having incurred your displeasure—to the despair of giving you affliction—to the unsufferable idea of being unworthy of you? Your mind is taken up with punishing, whilst I languish for consolation; not that I deserve it, but only that I am in want of it, and that it is you alone can console me.

If on a sudden, forgetful of our mutual love as of my happiness, you will abandon me to perpetual sorrow, I shall not dispute your right—strike: but should you incline to indulgence, and again recall those tender sentiments that united our hearts; that voluptuousness of soul, ever renewing, ever increasing; those delightful days we passed together; all the felicities that love only can give; you will, perhaps, prefer the power of renewing to that of destroying them. What shall I say? I have lost all, and lost it by my own folly: but still all may be retrieved by your goodness. You are now to decide. I shall add but one word more. Yesterday you swore my happiness was certain whilst it depended on you. Ah! will you this day, then, Madam, give me up to everlasting despair?

Paris, Nov. 15, 17—.

LETTER CXXXVIII
VISCOUNT DE VALMONT to the
MARCHIONESS DE MERTEUIL

I insist on it, my charming friend, I am not in love; and it is not my fault, if circumstances oblige me to play the character of a lover.—Only consent to return, and you will be able to judge my sincerity—I made my proofs yesterday, and cannot be injured by what happens to-day.

I was with the tender prude, having nothing else to do; for the little Volanges, nothwithstanding her situation, was to spend the night at Madame de V— —'s early ball: the want of business first gave me an inclination to prolong the evening; and I had, with this intention, even required a little sacrifice: it was scarcely granted, than the pleasure I promised myself was disturbed with the idea of this love which you so obstinately will have it, or at least reproach me with being infected; so I determined at once to be certain myself, and convince you, that it was a calumny of your own.

In consequence I took a violent resolution; on a very slight pretence, I took leave, and left my fair one quite surprised, and doubtless more afflicted, while I quietly went to meet Emily at the opera: she can satisfy you, that until morning, when we parted, no regret disturbed our amusements.

Yet there was a pretty large field for uneasiness, if my total indifference had not preserved me: for you must know, I was scarce four houses from the opera, with Emily in my carriage, when that of the austere devotee ranged close beside mine, and a stop which happened, left us near half a quarter of an hour close by each other; we could see one another as plain as at noon day, and there was no means to escape.

That is not all; I took it in my head to tell Emily confidentially, that was the letter-woman. You may recollect, perhaps, that piece of folly, and that Emily was the desk[1]. She did not forget it, and as she laughs immoderately, she was not easy until she had attentively viewed this piece of virtue, as she called her; and with scandalous bursts, such as would even disconcert effrontery.

Still this is not all; the jealous woman sent to my house that same night; I was not at home, but she obstinately sent a second time, with orders to wait my return. I sent my carriage home, as soon as I resolved to spend the night with Emily, without any other orders to my coachman, than to return this morning. When he got home he found the messenger, whom he informed I was not to return that night. You may guess the effect of this news, and that at my return, I found my discharge announced with all the dignity the circumstance required.

Thus, this adventure, which according to your opinion, was never to be determined, could, as you see, have been ended this morning? if it should not, I would not have you think I prize a continuance of it; but I do not think it consistent with my character to be quitted: moreover, I intend to reserve the honour of this sacrifice for you.

I have answered her severe note with a long sentimental epistle; I have given long reasons, and rely on love to make them acceptable. I have already succeeded—I have received a second note, still very rigorous, and which confirms an everlasting rupture, as it ought to be—but the ton is not the same; I must not be seen again; this resolution is announced four times in the most irrevocable manner. From thence I concluded, there was not a moment to be lost in presenting myself: I have already sent my huntsman to secure the porter, and shall follow instantly, to have my pardon sealed: for in crimes of this nature, there is only one form for a general absolution, and that must be executed in each others presence.

Adieu, my charming friend! I fly to achieve this grand event.

Paris, Nov. 15, 17—.

[1] Letters xlvi and xlvii.

LETTER CXXXIX
The Presidente DE TOURVEL to MADAME DE ROSEMONDE

How I reproach myself, my dear friend, for having wrote too soon, and said too much of my transitory troubles! I am the cause you at present are afflicted; the chagrin I have given you still continues, and I am happy; yes, every thing is forgot, and I forgive; or rather all is cleared up. Calm and delight succeed this state of grief and anguish; how shall I express the ecstasy of my heart! Valmont is innocent: with so much love there can be no guilt—those heavy offensive crimes with which I loaded him so bitterly, he did not deserve; and although I was right in one single point, yet I was to make reparation for my unjust suspicions.

I will not relate minutely the circumstances of facts or reasonings in his justification—Perhaps even the mind would but badly appreciate them—it is the heart only can feel them. However, were you even to suspect me of weakness, I would call on your judgment in support of my own; you say among men infidelity is not inconstancy.

Not but I am sensible, this opinion, which custom authorises, hurts delicacy: but why should mine complain, when Valmont's suffers more? This same injury which I forget, I do not think he forgives himself; and yet he has immensely repaired this trivial error, by the excess of his love, and my happiness!

My felicity is greater, or I know the value of it better, since my dread of losing him; I can aver to you, if I had strength sufficient to undergo again such cruel chagrins as I have just experienced, I should not think I had purchased my increase of happiness at too high a rate. Oh, my dear mother! scold your unthinking daughter for afflicting you by her precipitation; scold her for having rashly judged him she should ever adore; and knowing her imprudence, see her happy: augment her bliss by partaking it.

Paris, Nov. 15, 17—.

LETTER CXL
The VISCOUNT DE VALMONT to the MARCHIONESS DE MERTEUIL

How comes it, my charming friend, I receive no answers from you? I think, however, my last letter deserved one; these three days have I been expecting it, and must still wait! I really am vexed, and shall not relate a syllable of my grand affairs.

Such as the reconciliation had its full effect: that instead of reproaches and dissidence, it produced fresh proofs of affection; that I now actually receive the excuse and satisfaction due to my suspected candour; not a word shall you know—had it not been for the unforeseen event of last night, I should not have wrote to you at all; but as it relates to your pupil, who probably cannot give you any information herself, at least for some time, I have taken upon me to acquaint you with it.

For reasons you may or may not guess, Madame de Tourvel, has not engaged my attention for some days: as those reasons could not exist with the little Volanges, I became more assiduous there. Thanks to the obliging porter, I had no obstacles to surmount; and your pupil and I led a comfortable, regular life—Custom brings on negligence; at first we had not taken proper precautions for our security; we trembled behind the locks: yesterday an incredible absence of mind occasioned the accident I am going to relate; as to myself, fear was my only punishment, but the little girl did not come off so well.

We were not asleep, but reposing in the abandonment consequent to voluptuousness, when on a sudden, we heard the room door open, I instantly seized my sword to defend myself and our pupil; I advanced, and saw no one; but the door was open: as we had a light, I examined all about the room, and did not find a mortal; then I recollected we had forgot our usual precautions, and certainly the door being only pushed or not properly shut, opened of itself.

Returning to my terrified companion to quiet her, I did not find her in the bed; she fell out, or hid herself by the bedside; at length I found her there, stretched senseless on the ground, in strong convulsions—You may judge my embarrassment—However, I brought her to herself, and got her into bed again, but she had hurt herself in the fall, and was not long before she felt its effect.

Pains in the loins, violent cholics, and other symptoms less equivocal, soon informed me her condition—To make her sensible of it, it was necessary to acquaint her with the one she was in before, of which she had not the least suspicion: never any one before her, perhaps, went to work so innocently to get rid of it—she does not lose her time in reflection.

But she lost a great deal in afflicting herself, and I found it necessary to come to some resolution: therefore we agreed I should immediately go to the physician and surgeon of the family, to inform them they would be sent for; I was to make them a confidence of the whole business, under a promise of secrecy—That she should ring for her waiting maid, and should or should not make her a confidence of her situation, as she thought proper; but at all events, send for assistance, and should forbid her from disturbing Madame de Volanges. An attentive delicacy natural to a girl who feared to give her mother uneasiness.

I made my two visits and confessions as expeditiously as I could, and then went home, from whence I have not since stirred. The surgeon, who I knew before, came to me at noon, to give me an account of the state of his patient—I was not mistaken—He hopes, however, it will not be attended with any bad consequences. Provided no accident happens, it will not be discovered in the house; the waiting woman is in the secret; the physician has given the disorder a name, and this affair will be settled as a thousand others have been, unless hereafter it might be useful to us to have it mentioned.

Have you and I mutual interests or no? Your silence makes me dubious of it; I would not even think at all of it, if my inclinations did not lead me on to every method of preserving the hope of it. Adieu, my charming friend! yet in anger.

Paris, Nov. 21, 17—.

LETTER CXLI
The MARCHIONESS DE MERTEUIL
to the VISCOUNT DE VALMONT

Good God, Viscount! How troublesome you are with your obstinacy! What matters my silence to you? Do you believe it is for want of reasons I am silent? Ah! would to God! But no, it is only because it would be painful to tell them to you.

Speak truth, do you deceive yourself, or do you mean to deceive me? The difference between your discourse and actions, leaves in doubt which I am to give credit to. What shall I say to you then, when I even do not know what to think?

You seem to make a great merit of your last scene with the Presidente; but what does that prove in support of your system, or against mine? I never certainly told you, your love for this woman was so violent as not be capable of deceiving her, or prevent you from enjoying every opportunity that appeared agreeable and easy to you. I never even doubted but it would be equally the same to you, to satisfy, with any other, the first that offered, the desires she would raise. I am not at all surprised, that from a libertinism of mind, which it would be wrong to contend with you, you have once done designedly, what you have a thousand times done occasionally—Don't we well know this is the way of the world, and the practice of you all? and whoever acts otherwise is looked on as a simpleton—I think I don't charge you with this defect.

What I have said, what I have thought, what I still think, is, you are nevertheless in love with your Presidente: not if you will with a pure and tender passion, but of that kind of which you are capable; for example, of that kind which makes you discover in a woman, charms and qualities she has not: which ranks her in a class by herself, and still links you to her even while you insult her—Such, in a word, as a Sultan has for a favourite Sultana; that does not prevent him from often giving the preference to a plain Odalisk. My comparison appears to me the more just, as, like him, you never are the lover or friend of a woman, but always her tyrant or her slave. And I am very certain, you very much humbled and debased yourself very much, to get into favour again with this fine object! Happy in your success, as soon as you think the moment arrived to obtain your pardon, you leave me *for this grand event.*

Even in your last letter, the reason you give for not entertaining me solely with this woman is, because you will not tell me any thing of your *grand affairs*; they are of so much importance, that your silence on that subject is to be my punishment: and after giving me such strong proofs of a decided preference for another, you coolly ask me whether *we have a mutual interest!* Have a care, Viscount; if I once answer you, my answer shall be irrevocable: and to be in suspense, is perhaps saying too much; I will therefore now say no more of that matter.

I have nothing more to say, but to tell you a trifling story; perhaps you will not have leisure to read it, or to give so much attention to it as to understand it properly? At worst, it will be only a tale thrown away.

A man of my acquaintance, like you, was entangled with a woman, who did him very little credit; he had sense enough, at times, to perceive, this adventure would hurt him one time or other—Although he was ashamed of it, yet he had not the resolution to break off—His embarrassment was greater, as he had frequently boasted to his friends, he was entirely at liberty; and was not insensible, the more he apologised, the more the ridicule increased—Thus, he spent his time incessantly in foolery, and constantly saying, *it is not my fault.* This man had a friend, who was one time very near giving him up in his frenzy to indelible ridicule: but yet, being more generous than malicious, or perhaps from some other motive, she resolved, as a last effort, to try a method to be able, at least, with her friend, to say, *it is not my fault.* She therefore sent him, without farther ceremony, the following letter, as a remedy for his disorder.

"One tires of every thing, my angel! It is a law of nature; it is not my fault.

"If, then, I am tired of a connection that has entirely taken me up four long months, it is not my fault.

"If, for example, I had just as much love as you had virtue, and that's saying a great deal, it is not at all surprising that one should end with the other; it is not my fault.

"It follows, then, that for some time past, I have deceived you; but your unmerciful affection in some measure forced me to it! It is not my fault.

"Now a woman I love to distraction, insists I must sacrifice you: it is not my fault.

"I am sensible here is a fine field for reproaches; but if nature has only granted men constancy, whilst it gives obstinacy to women, it is not my fault.

"Take my advice, choose another lover, as I have another mistress—The advice is good; if you think otherwise, it is not my fault.

"Farewell, my angel! I took you with pleasure, I part you without regret; perhaps I shall return to you; it is the way of the world; it is not my fault."

This is not the time to tell you, Viscount, the effect of this last effort, and its consequences; but I promise to give it you in my next letter; you will then receive also my ultimatum on renewing the treaty you propose. Until when, adieu.

Now I think on it, receive my thanks for your particular account of the little Volanges; that article will keep till the day after her wedding, for the scandalous gazette. I condole with you, however, on the loss of your progeny. Good night, Viscount.

Nov. 24, 17—. Castle of ——.

LETTER CXLII
VISCOUNT DE VALMONT to the MARCHIONESS DE MERTEUIL

I don't know, my charming friend, whether I have read or understood badly your letter, the little tale you relate, and the epistolary model it contains—But this I must say, the last is an original, and seems very proper to take effect; therefore I only copied it, and sent it without farther ceremony to the celestial Presidente. I did not lose a moment, for the tender epistle was dispatched yesterday evening—I chose to act so; for first, I had promised to write to her; and, moreover, I thought a whole night not too much for her to collect herself, and ruminate on *this grand event*, were you even to reproach me a second time with the expression.

I expected to have sent you back this morning my well-beloved's answer; it is now near twelve, and it is not yet come—I shall wait until five; and if I receive no news by that time, I shall in person seek it, for every thing must be done according to form, and the difficulty is only in this first step.

Now you may believe I am impatient to know the end of your story of that man of your acquaintance, who was so violently suspected of not knowing how to sacrifice a woman upon occasion—Did he not amend, and did not his generous friend forgive him?

I am no less anxious to receive your ultimatum as you call it so politically; but I am curious, above all, to know if you can perceive any impression of love in this last proceeding? Ah! doubtless there is, and a good deal! But for whom? Still I make no pretensions; I expect every thing from your goodness.

Adieu, charmer! I shall not close my letter until two, in hope of adding the wished-for answer.

Two o'clock in the afternoon.

Nothing yet—the time slips away; I can't spare a moment—but surely now you will not refuse the tenderest kisses of love.

Paris, Nov. 27, 17—.

LETTER CXLIII
The Presidente DE TOURVEL to MADAME DE ROSEMONDE

The veil is rent, Madam, on which was painted my illusory happiness—The fatal truth is cleared, that leaves me no prospect but an assured and speedy death; and my road is traced between shame and remorse. I will follow it—I will cherish my torments if they will shorten my existence—I send you the letter I received yesterday; it needs no reflections; it contains them all—This is not a time for lamentation—nothing remains but sufferings—I want not pity, I want strength.

Receive, Madame, the only adieu I shall make, and grant my last request: leave me to my fate—forget me totally—do not reckon me among the living. There is a limit in misery, when even friendship augments our sufferings and cannot cure them—When wounds are mortal, all relief is cruel. Every sentiment but despair is foreign to my soul—nothing can now suit me, but the darkness where I am going to bury my shame—There will I weep crimes, if I yet can weep; for since yesterday I have not shed a tear—my withered heart no longer furnishes any.

Adieu, Madame! Do not reply to this—I have taken a solemn oath on this letter never to receive another.

Paris, Nov. 27, 17—.

LETTER CXLIV
VISCOUNT DE VALMONT to the
MARCHIONESS DE MERTEUIL

Yesterday, at three in the afternoon, being impatient, my lovely friend, at not having any news, I presented myself at the house of the fair abandoned, and was told she was gone out. In this reply I could see nothing more than a refusal to admit me, which neither surprised nor vexed me; I retired, in hope this step would induce so polished a woman to give me an answer. The desire I had to receive one, made me call home about nine, but found nothing. Astonished at this silence, which I did not expect, I sent my huntsman on the enquiry for information, whether the tender fair was dead or dying. At my return, he informed me, Madame de Tourvel had actually gone out at eleven in the morning with her waiting maid; that she ordered her carriage to the convent of — —; that at seven in the evening she had sent her carriage and servants back, sending word they should not expect her home. This is certainly acting with propriety. The convent is the only asylum for a widow; and if she persists in so laudable a resolution, I shall add to all the obligations I already lay under, the celebrity this adventure will now have.

I told you sometime ago, notwithstanding your uneasiness, I would again appear in the world with more brilliant eclat. Let those severe critics now show themselves, who accused me of a romantic passion; let them make a more expeditious and shining rupture: no, let them do more; bid them go offer their consolations—the road is chalked out for them; let them only dare run the career I have gone over entirely, and if any one obtains the least success, I will yield him up the first place: but they shall all experience when I am in earnest; the impression I leave is indelible. This one I affirm will be so. I should even look on all former triumphs as trifles, if I was ever to have a favoured rival.

I own the step she has taken flatters my vanity; yet I am sorry she had so much fortitude to separate from me. There will be no obstacle, then, between us, but of my own formation. If I should be inclined to renew our connection, she, perhaps, would refuse; perhaps not pant for it, not think it the summit of happiness! Is this love? And do you think, my charming friend, I should bear it? Could I not, for example, and would it not be better, endeavour to bring this woman to the point of foreseeing a possibility of a reconciliation, always wished for while there is hope? I could try this course without any consequence, without giving you umbrage. It would be only a mere trial we would make in concert. Even if I should be successful, it would be only an additional means of renewing, at your pleasure, a sacrifice which has seemed agreeable to you. Now, my charming friend, I am yet to receive my reward, and all my vows are for your return. Come, then, speedily to your lover, your pleasures, your friends, and the pursuit of adventures.

That of the little Volanges has had a surprising turn. Yesterday, as my uneasiness would not suffer me to stay long in a place, in my various excursions I called at Madame Volanges's. I found your pupil in the saloon, in the drapery of a sick person, but in full health, fresher, and more interesting. Some of you ladies, in such a case would keep your beds for a month, Oh, rare lasses! Egad, this one has given me a strong inclination to know if the cure be complete.

I had almost forgot to tell you, the little girl's accident had like to have turned your *sentimental* Danceny's brain: at first it was for grief, but now it is with joy. *His Cecilia* was sick. You will agree, the brain must turn with such a misfortune. Three times a day did he send to enquire about her, and never missed every day going himself; at last, he wrote a fine epistle to the mama, begging leave to go and congratulate her on the recovery of so dear an object; Madame de Volanges assented; so that I found the young man established as heretofore, only not quite so familiar. This narrative I had from himself; for I came out with him, and made him prate. You can't conceive what an effect this visit had on him; his joy, his wishes, his transports are inexpressible. As I am fond of grand emotions, I finished him, by telling him, in a few days I hoped to place him much nearer his fair one.

I am determined to give her up to him as soon as I have made my trial. I will devote myself entirely to you; moreover, I don't see it would be worth while your pupil should be my scholar, if she had only a husband to deceive. The *chef d'œuvre* is to deceive the lover! and the first lover too! For I can't reproach myself with even having pronounced the word love.

Adieu, my lovely friend! Return as soon as possible to resume your empire over me, to receive my homage, and give me my reward.

Paris, Nov. 28, 17—.

LETTER CXLV
The MARCHIONESS DE MERTEUIL to the VISCOUNT DE VALMONT

Now seriously, Viscount, have you left the Presidente? Did you send her the letter I wrote you for her? You are a charming fellow, indeed, and have surpassed my expectations! I must own, this triumph flatters me more than all those I ever obtained. You will think, perhaps, I estimate this woman very highly, who I depreciated very lately; not in the least: but it is not over her this advantage is gained; it is over you; there lies the jest, and it is really delightful.

Yes, Viscount, you loved Madame de Tourvel much, and you still love her; you love her to distraction: but because I made you ashamed, by way of amusement, you nobly sacrifice her. You would have sacrificed a thousand women rather than be laughed at. To what lengths will not vanity lead us! The wise man was right when he said it was the foe to happiness.

What would become of you now, if it had been only a trick I put upon you? But I am incapable of deceit, and you know it well; and should you even in my turn reduce me to despair and a convent, I will risk it, and surrender to my conqueror. Still, if I do capitulate, upon my word it is from mere frailty; for were I inclined, how many cavils could I not start! and, perhaps, you would deserve them!

I admire, for example, with how much address, or awkwardness rather, you soothingly propose I should let you renew with your Presidente. It would be very convenient, would it not? to take all the merit of this rapture without losing the pleasure of enjoyment! And then this proffered sacrifice, which would no longer be one to you, is offered to be renewed at my pleasure! By this arrangement, the celestial devotee would always think herself the only choice of your heart, whilst I should wrap myself up in the pride of being the preferred rival; we should both be deceived; you would be satisfied: all the rest is of no consequence.

It is much to be lamented, that with such extraordinary talents for projects, you have so few for execution; and that by one inconsiderate step, you put an insurmountable obstacle to what you so much wished.

What! you had, then, an idea of renewing your connection, and yet you copied my letter! You must, then, have thought me awkward indeed! Believe me, Viscount, when a woman strikes at the heart of another, she seldom misses her blow, and the wound is incurable. When I struck this one, or rather directed the blow, I did not forget she was my rival, that you had for a moment preferred her to me, placed me beneath her. If I am deceived in my revenge, I consent to bear the blame; therefore, I agree you may attempt every means; even I invite you to it, and promise you I shall not be angry at your success. I am so easy on this matter, I shall say no more of it: let us talk of something else.

As to the health of the little Volanges, you will be able to give me some positive news at my return. I shall be glad to have some. After that, you will be the best judge whether it will be most convenient to give the little girl up to her lover, or endeavour to be the founder of a new branch of the Valmonts, under the name of Gercourt. This idea pleases me much: but in leaving the choice to yourself, I must yet require you will not come to a definitive resolution until we talk the matter over. It is not putting you off for a long time, for I shall be in Paris immediately. I can't positively say the day; but be assured, as soon as I arrive, you shall be the first informed of it.

Adieu, Viscount! notwithstanding my quarrels, my mischievousness, and my reproaches, I always love you much, and am preparing to prove it. Adieu, till our next meeting.

Castle of — —, Nov. 29, 17—.

LETTER CXLVI
The MARCHIONESS DE MERTEUIL
to the CHEVALIER DANCENY

At last I set out, my young friend; to-morrow evening I shall be in Paris. The hurry always attending a removal will prevent me from seeing any one. Yet if you should have any pressing confidential business to impart, I shall except you from the general rule: but I except you alone; therefore request my arrival may be a secret. I shall not even inform Valmont of it.

Whoever would have told me, sometime ago, you would have my exclusive confidence, I would not have believed them: but yours drew on mine. I should be inclined to think you had made use of some address, or, perhaps, seduction. That would be wrong, indeed! however, it would not at present be very dangerous; you have other business in hand. When the heroine is on the stage, we seldom take notice of the confidant.

And, indeed, you have not had time to impart your late success to me. When your Cecilia was absent, the days were too short to listen to your plaintive strains. You would have told them to the echo, if I had not been ready to hear them. Since, when she was ill, you even honoured me with a recital of your troubles; you wanted some one to tell them to: but now your love is in Paris, that she is quite recovered, and you sometimes see her, your friends are quite neglected.

I do not blame you in the least, it is a fault of youth; for it is a received truth, that from Alcibiades down to you, young people are unacquainted with friendship but in adversity. Happiness sometimes makes them indiscreet, but never presumptuous. I will say, with Socrates, *I like my friends to come to me when they are unhappy:* but, as a philosopher, he did very well without them if they did not come. I am not quite so wise as he, for I felt your silence with all the weakness of a woman.

However, do not think me too exacting; far from it. The same sentiment that leads me to observe those privations, makes me bear them with fortitude, when they are proofs, or the cause of the happiness of my friends. I shall, therefore, not depend on you for to-morrow evening, only as far as is consistent with love and want of occupation; and I positively forbid you to make me the least sacrifice.

Adieu, Chevalier! it will be an absolute regale to see you again—will you come?

Castle of — —, Nov. 29, 17—.

LETTER CXLVII
MADAME DE VOLANGES to
MADAME DE ROSEMONDE

You will most assuredly be as much afflicted, my dear friend, as I am, when I acquaint you with Madame de Tourvel's state; she has been indisposed since yesterday: she was taken so suddenly, and her disorder is of such an alarming nature, that I am really frightened about it.

A burning fever, an almost constant and violent delirium, a perpetual thirst, are the symptoms. The physicians say, they cannot as yet form their prognostics; and their endeavours are frustrated, as the patient obstinately refuses every kind of remedy: insomuch, that they were obliged to use force to bleed her; and were twice since forced to use the same method, to tie up the bandages, which she tore off in her fits.

You and I, who have seen her, so weak, so timid, so mild, could hardly conceive that four persons scarcely could hold her; and on the least remonstrance she flies out in the greatest rage imaginable: for my part, I fear it is something worse than a raving, and borders on downright madness.

And what happened the day before yesterday adds to my fears.

On that day she came about eleven in the morning to the convent of — — with her waiting maid. As she was educated in that house, and occasionally came to visit there, she was received as usual, and appeared to every one in good health and very quiet. In about two hours after she asked, whether the room she had, whilst she was a pensioner, was vacant? and being answered in the affirmative, she begged leave to see it; the prioress and some of the nuns accompanied her. She then declared she came back to settle in this room, which, said she, I ought never to have quitted; adding, she would not depart from it *until death:* that was her expression.

At first, they stared at each other: but the first surprise being over, they remonstrated, that, as a married woman, she could not be received without a special permission. That, and a thousand other arguments were unavailable; and from that moment she was obstinate, not only to remain in the convent, but even not to stir from the room. At length, being tired out, they consented, at seven in the evening, she should remain there that night. Her carriage and servants were sent home, and they adjourned until the next day.

I have been assured, during the whole night her appearance and deportment did not exhibit the least wandering symptom; on the contrary, she seemed composed and deliberate; only fell into a profound reverie four or five times, which conversation could not remove; and every time before she recovered from it, she seemed forcibly to squeeze her forehead with both hands: on which one of the nuns asked her if she had a pain in her head; she fixed her eyes on her sometime before she replied, and said, "My disorder is not there." Immediately after she begged to be left alone, and also, that in future they should not put any questions to her.

Every one retired except her waiting maid, who was fortunately obliged to sleep in the same chamber.

According to the girl's account, her mistress was pretty quiet until about eleven at night; then she said she would go to bed: but before she was quite undressed, she walked to and fro in her room with much action and gesture. Julie, who was present at every thing that passed during the day, did not dare say a word, and silently waited near an hour. At length, Madame de Tourvel called her twice on a sudden; she had scarce time to reach her, when her mistress dropped in her arms, saying, "I can hold out no longer." She suffered her to lead her to her bed; but would not take any thing, nor allow her to call for assistance. She ordered her only to leave her some water, and go to bed.

The girl avers, she did not go to sleep till two in the morning, and heard neither disturbance nor complaint. At five she was awoke by her mistress, who spoke in a strong loud tone. She asked, if she wanted any thing; but receiving no answer, she went to Madame de Tourvel's bedside with a light, who did not know her; but breaking off her incoherent discourse, exclaimed violently, "Leave me alone! Let me be left in darkness! It is darkness alone suits me!" I remarked yesterday, she often repeated those expressions.

At last, Julie took this opportunity to go out and call for assistance, which Madame de Tourvel refused with the greatest fury and madness. These fits have often returned since.

The distress the whole convent was thrown in, induced the Prioress to send for me yesterday morning at seven, when it was not yet day. I went immediately. When I was announced to Madame de Tourvel, she seemed to come to herself, and said, "Ah! yes, let her come in." She fixed her eyes on me when I came near her bed, and seizing my hand suddenly, she squeezed it, saying, in a strong, melancholy tone, "I die for not having taken your advice;" and immediately covering her eyes, she resumed her delirium of "Leave me alone," &c. and lost all reason.

Those discourses, and some others that fell from her in her delirium, make me apprehend this dreadful disorder has still a more cruel cause; but let us respect the secrets of our friend, and pity her misfortune.

All yesterday was equally stormy, either fits of frightful deliriousness, or lethargic faintness, the only time when she takes or gives any rest. I did not leave her bed's head until nine at night, and am going again this morning for the day.

I will not certainly abandon our unhappy friend: but her obstinacy in refusing all help and assistance is very distressing.

I enclose you the journal of last night, which I have just received, and which, as you will see, brings but little consolation. I will take care to send them you regularly.

Adieu, my worthy friend! I am going to visit our poor friend. My daughter, who is perfectly recovered, presents her compliments to you.

Paris, Nov. 29, 17—.

LETTER CXLVIII
The CHEVALIER DANCENY to the MARCHIONESS DE MERTEUIL

O you, whom I love! O thou, whom I adore! O you, with whom my happiness hath commenced! O thou, who hast completed it! Compassionate friend! tender mistress! why does the reflection that you are a prey to grief come to disturb my charmed mind? Ah, Madam! resume your calmness; it is the duty of friendship to make this entreaty. O my heart's only object! be happy; it is the prayer of love.

What reproaches have you to make to yourself? Believe me, your extraordinary delicacy misleads you. The regret it occasions you, the injuries it charges me with, are equally imaginary; and I feel within my heart, that there has been between us no other seducer than love. No longer dread, then, to yield to those sentiments you inspire, or to partake of a flame you have kindled. What! would we have had more reason to boast of purity in our connection, if it had taken more time to form? Undoubtedly not. That is the characteristic of seduction, which, never acting unless by projects, is able to regulate its progress and means, and foresees events at a great distance: but true love does not permit that kind of meditation and reflection; it diverts us from thought with occupying us wholly with sentiments. Its empire is never more powerful than when unknown; and it is in obscurity and silence that it steals upon us, and binds us in chains equally impossible to be perceived or to be broken.

Thus, even yesterday, notwithstanding the lively emotions which the idea of your return caused in me, in defiance of the extreme pleasure I felt on seeing you, I nevertheless thought myself led and called upon by serene friendship alone, or rather entirely absorbed by the sweet sentiments of my heart, I concerned myself very little in tracing either their cause or origin. Like me, my dear friend, you experienced, though unconscious of it, that all-powerful charm, which gave up our whole souls to the rapturous impression of tenderness, and neither of us recognised it to be love, till after the intoxication that deity plunged us into.

But that very circumstance is our exculpation, instead of our guilt. No, you did not betray the rights of friendship, nor have I abused your confidence. We both, it is true, were ignorant of our sentiments; but we only underwent the delusion, without any efforts to give birth to it: and far from complaining of it, let us only think of the happiness it procured us, without disturbing it by unjust reproaches; let our only endeavours be to farther augment it, by the pleasures of confidence and entire security. O, my friend! how dear these hopes are to my heart! Yes, henceforward freed from all fears, and wholly occupied by love, you will participate of my desires, of my transports, of the sweet delirium of my senses, of the intoxication of my soul, and each moment of our happy days shall be marked by a new enjoyment.

Adieu, thou whom I adore! I shall see thee this evening; but shall I find you alone? I hardly dare to hope it. Ah! you do not desire it as much as I!

Paris, Dec. 1, 17—.

LETTER CXLIX
MADAME DE VOLANGES to MADAME DE ROSEMONDE

I was in hopes almost all day yesterday, to have been able to give you, my worthy friend, this morning, a more favourable account of our dear patient; but since last night, that hope is utterly destroyed. A matter seemingly of very little importance, but which, in its consequences, proves to be a very unhappy one, has made the case at least as grievous as before, if not worse.

I should not have had any comprehension of this sudden change, if I had not received yesterday the entire confidence of our unhappy friend. As she did not conceal from me that you also are acquainted with all her misfortunes, I can inform you every thing without reserve of her unhappy situation.

Yesterday morning, on my arrival at the convent, I was informed she had been asleep about three hours; and that sleep, so profound and so easy, I for some time was apprehensive was lethargic—Some time after she awoke, and opened the curtains of the bed herself.

At first she looked at us all with great surprise, and as I rose to go to her, she knew me, called me by my name, and begged I would come near her. She did not give me time to ask her any questions, but desired to know where she was; what we were doing there; if she was sick; and why she was not in her own house? I imagined at first, it was another frenzy, only more gentle than the former: but I soon perceived she understood my replies perfectly; and she had recovered her reason, but not her memory.

She questioned me very minutely on every thing that happened to her since she came to the convent, which she did not remember. I gave her a faithful account, only concealing what I thought might frighten her too much: and when I asked how she was, she replied she did not then feel any pain: but was much tormented during her sleep, and found herself fatigued. I advised her to keep quiet, and say little: then I partly closed the curtains, and sat down by the side of her bed: some broth was then proposed, which she agreed to take, and liked it very well.

She continued thus about half an hour, and only spoke to thank me for my care of her, which she did with that graceful ease you know is so natural to her; afterwards she was for some time quite silent, which she broke at length, saying, "O yes, I now remember my coming here;" and a minute after, exclaimed grievously, "My dear friend, have pity on me! My miseries are all returning on me." I was then coming towards her, she grasped my hand, and leaning her head against it, "Great God!" said she, "cannot I then die!" Her expression more than her words melted me into tears; she perceived it by my voice, and said, "you pity me then; ah, if you but knew!"—Then breaking off: "Let us be alone, and I will tell you all."

I believe I already wrote to you I had some suspicions, which I was apprehensive would be the topic of this conversation that I foresaw would be tedious and melancholy, and might probably be very detrimental to the present state of our unhappy friend. I endeavoured to dissuade her from it, by urging the necessity of repose; she however, insisted, and I was obliged to acquiesce.

As soon as we were alone, she acquainted me with every thing you already know, therefore unnecessary to be repeated.

At last, relating the cruel manner in which she was sacrificed, she added, "I was very certain it would be my death, and I was resolved—but it is impossible to survive my shame and grief." I attempted to contend against this depression, or rather despair, with motives of a religious nature, always hitherto so powerful in her mind; but I was soon convinced I was not equal to this solemn function, and I determined to propose calling in Father Anselmus, in whom I knew she reposes great confidence. She consented, and even appeared much to desire it—He was sent for, and came immediately: he stayed a long time with her, and said, going away, if the physicians were of the same opinion he was, the ceremony of the sacraments he thought might be postponed until the day following.

This was about three in the afternoon, and our friend was pretty quiet until five, so that we all began to conceive some hope; but unfortunately a letter was then brought for her; when it was offered to her, she replied at first she would not receive any, and no one pressed it; but from that time she seemed more disturbed. Soon after she asked from whom the letter came?—It had no post-mark—Who brought it?—No one knew—From what place did the messenger say it came?—The portress was not informed. She remained silent some time after; then again began to speak; but her discourse was so incoherent, we were soon convinced the frenzy was returned.

However there was a quiet interval afterwards, until at last she desired the letter should be given to her. The moment she cast her eyes on it, she exclaimed, "Good God! from him!" and then in a strong and oppressed tone of voice, "Take it, take it." She instantly ordered the curtains of her bed to be closed, and desired no one should come near her; but we were all soon obliged to come round her: the frenzy returned with more violence than ever, accompanied with most dreadful convulsions—Those shocking incidents continued the whole evening; and the account I received this morning, informs me, the night has been no less turbulent. On the whole, I am astonished she has held out so long in the condition she is: and I will not conceal from you, that I have very little, if any, hope of her recovery.

I suppose this unfortunate letter is from M. de Valmont—What! can he still dare to write to her! Forgive me, my dear friend; I must put a stop to my reflections—It is, however, a most cruel case, to see a woman make so wretched an end, who has, until now, lived so happy, and was so worthy being so.

Paris, Dec. 2, 17—.

LETTER CL
CHEVALIER DANCENY to the MARCHIONESS DE MERTEUIL

In expectation of the happiness of seeing you, I indulge myself, my tender friend, in the pleasure of writing to you; and thus by occupying myself with you, I dispel the gloom that otherwise would be occasioned by your absence. To delineate to you my sentiments, to recall yours to my mind, is a true enjoyment to my heart; and thus even the time of privation affords me a thousand ideas precious to my love—Yet, if I am to believe you, I shall not obtain any answer from you, even this letter shall be the last, and we shall abandon a correspondence which, according to you, is dangerous, *and of which we have no need*—Certainly I shall believe you if you persist; for what can you desire that does not of course become my desire? But before you ultimately decide upon it, will you not permit a slight conversation on the subject.

Of the head of danger you are the only judge—I can frame no calculation of it—and I shall confine myself to requesting you would look to your own safety, for I can have no tranquillity while you are disquieted—As to this object, it is not we two that are but one, it is thou that art us both.

As to the matter of necessity, we can have but one thought; and if we differ in opinion, it can only rise from a want of proper explanation, or from not understanding one another. I shall therefore state to you what I think is my sensation.

Without doubt a letter appears very unnecessary when we can see one another freely—What could it say that a word, or look, or even silence itself, could not express? A hundred times before, this appeared to me so clear, that in the very moment that you spoke to me of not writing any more, that idea my mind immediately adopted—It was a restraint upon it perhaps, but did not affect it—Thus, when I have offered a kiss upon your bosom, and found a ribband or piece of gauze in my way, I only turn it aside, and have not the least sentiment of an obstacle.

But since we have separated, and you are no longer there, this idea of correspondence by letters has returned to torment me—What is the reason,

I have said to myself, of this additional privation? Why is it, because we are at some distance, we have nothing more to say to each other? Suppose that a fortunate concurrence of circumstances should bring us together for a day, shall we then employ in conversation the time that ought to be wholly dedicated to enjoyment, which letters between us would prevent? I say enjoyment, my dear friend; for with you the very moments of repose furnish, too, a delicious enjoyment; in a word, whenever such a happy opportunity offers, the conclusion is still separation; and one is so solitary, it is then a letter becomes truly precious: if not read, it is sure to be the only object that employs the eye. Ah! there can be no doubt, but one may look at a letter without reading it; as I think that I even could have some pleasure at night by barely touching your portrait.

Your portrait have I said? but a letter is the portrait of the soul; it has not, like a cold image, that degree of stagnation so opposite to love; it yields to all our actions by turns; it becomes animated, gives us enjoyment, and sinks into repose—All your sentiments are precious to me; and will you deprive me of the means of becoming possessed of them?

Are you quite sure that a desire to write to me will never torment you? If in the midst of your solitude your heart should be too much compressed or desolated; if a joyous emotion should pass to your soul; if an involuntary sadness should disturb it for a moment, it would not then be in the bosom of your friend that you would pour out your happiness or distress; you would then have a sensation he should not share; and you would punish him to wander in solitude and distrust far from you. My friend, my dearest friend! you are to pronounce—I have only proposed to myself to discuss the question with you, and not to over-rule you—I have only offered you reasons—I dare hope I should have stood on stronger ground if I had proceeded to entreaties—I shall endeavour, then, if you should persist, not to be afflicted; I shall use my efforts to tell myself what you would have wrote to me; but you would tell it better than I, and I should have a much higher gratification in hearing it from you.

Adieu, my charming friend! The hour approaches at last, when I shall be able to see you: I fly from you with the more haste, in order the sooner to meet you again.

Paris, Dec. 3, 17—.

LETTER CLI
The VISCOUNT DE VALMONT to the MARCHIONESS DE MERTEUIL

Surely, Marchioness, you do not take me to be such a novice, to imagine I could be duped in the tête-à-tête which I found you in this afternoon; or by the *astonishing chance* that led Danceny to your house! Not but your well-practised countenance wonderfully assumed a calm serenity of expression; or that you, by the most trifling word, betrayed, which sometimes happens, the least disorder or uneasiness. I will even allow your submissive looks served you eminently; and could they have made themselves as well credited as readily understood, far from having or harbouring the least suspicion, I should not at all have doubted the great vexation this *troublesome trio* gave you. But to display to greater advantage those extraordinary talents, to ensure the success you promised yourself, to carry on the deception you intended, you should have formed your inexperienced lover with more care.

Since you have begun to educate youth, you should teach your pupils not to blush or be disconcerted at a little raillery; not to deny so warmly for one woman, the same charge which they so faintly excuse themselves in for all others; teach them also to learn to hear encomiums on their mistress, without enhancing them.

And if you permit them to fix their looks on you in the circle, let them be taught to disguise that glance of enjoyment which is so easy to discover, and which they so unskilfully blend with the glance of love—Then you will be able to exhibit them in your public exercises, and their behaviour will not do any prejudice to their sage institutrix. Even myself, happy to be able to contribute to your celebrity, will compose and publish the exercises to be performed in this new college.

But I am astonished, I must own, that you should have undertaken to treat me as a school-boy. O! with any other woman, what pleasure I should have in being revenged! How transcendent it would be to that she should think to deprive me of! Yes, it is for you alone I condescend to give preference to satisfaction rather than revenge: and do not think I am restrained by the least doubt or uncertainty—I know all.

You have been in Paris now four days, and each day Danceny has been with you, and you have not admitted any one but him—even this day your door was still close; and had your porter's assurance been equal to his mistress's, I should not have seen you: yet you wrote me I might depend on being the first informed of your arrival. Of that same arrival, the particular day of which could not be ascertained, although you was writing to me the eve of your departure—Can you deny those facts, or will you attempt to excuse them? They are both equally impossible; and still I keep my temper! Acknowledge here your power; be satisfied to have experienced it, but do not any longer abuse it. We know each other, Marchioness; that should be sufficient.

To-morrow you are to be out for the day you told me; be it so, if you really go out, and you think I shall know it: but you will be home in the evening; we shall not have too much time until the next day to settle our difficult reconciliation. Let me know, then, if it will be at your house, *or yonder*, we shall make our numerous reciprocal expiations. But no more of Danceny; your wrong head had filled itself with his idea, and I am willing to overlook this delirium of your fancy; but remember, from this moment, that what was only a whim, would become a decided preference. I am not tempered for such an humiliation, neither do I expect to receive it from you.

I even expect this sacrifice will be but trifling to you—If it should be a little troublesome, I think, however, I have set you a tolerable example! A sensible and lovely woman, who existed for me only, who, perhaps, at this instant, is expiring with love and grief, may well be worth a young scholar, who, if you will, wants neither wit or accomplishments, but is deficient in consistency.

Adieu, Marchioness! I say nothing of my sentiments for you; all I can do at present is not to scrutinize my heart. I wait your answer. Remember, the easier it is for you to make me forget the injury you have done me, the more a denial, even the least delay, would engrave it in indelible characters on my heart.

Paris, Dec. 3, 17—.

LETTER CLII
The MARCHIONESS DE MERTEUIL
to the VISCOUNT DE VALMONT

Take care, Viscount; have a little more regard for my extreme timidity. How do you think I can support the unsufferable idea of your indignation; but especially that I do not sink under the terror of your vengeance? particularly as you know, if you defamed me, it would be impossible for me to return the compliment. In vain should I babble; your existence would nevertheless be brilliant and peaceful: for what would you have to dread? Only to be under the necessity of retiring if you had an opportunity. But could one not live in a foreign country as well as here? And to sum up all, provided the court of France would let you be quiet in the one you choose to settle in, it would be only changing the field of your victories. After endeavouring to bring you back to your *sang froid* by these moral considerations, let us resume our own affairs.

You do not know, Viscount, the reasons I never married again. It was not, I assure you, for want of several advantageous matches being offered to me; it was solely that no one should have a right to control me. It was not even a dread of not being able to pursue my inclinations, for certainly, at all events, that I should have done: but it would have pained me if any one should even have a right to complain. On the whole, it was that I would not wish to deceive but for my own pleasure, and not through necessity. And behold you write me the most matrimonial letter it is possible to conceive! You tell me of the injuries I have committed, and the favours you have granted! I cannot conceive how it is possible to be indebted to one where nothing is due.

Now for the business. You found Danceny at my house, and you was displeased; be it so: but what conclusion do you draw from thence? Why, that it was the effect of chance, as I told you, or of my inclination, which I did not tell you. In the first instance, your letter is wrong; in the second, ridiculous. It was well worth the trouble of writing! But you are jealous, and jealousy never debates. Well, I will argue for you.

You have a rival, or you have not. If you have a rival, you must please, to obtain the preference over him; and if you have none, you must still please, to avoid having one. In all cases the same invariable conduct must be observed. Why, then, will you torment yourself?—And why torment me? Have you, then, lost the secret of being the most amiable? And are you no longer certain of your success? Come, come, Viscount, you do yourself injustice. But that is not the case, for I will not, even in your mind, have you give yourself so much uneasiness. You wish less for my condescension, than an opportunity of abusing your power. Fie! you are very ungrateful! I think this is tolerably sentimental; and was I to continue any time, this letter might become very tender: but you don't deserve it.

Neither do you deserve I should enter farther in my justification. To punish you for your suspicions, you shall keep them; so that I shall make no reply as to the time of my return, or Danceny's visits. You have taken great trouble to be informed of them, most certainly: and pray what progress have you made by it? I hope you received great pleasure from your enquiries; as to mine, it has not been in the least detrimental to them.

All I can say, then, to your threatening letter is this—it has neither the gift of pleasing, nor power to intimidate me; and that at this present time I am not in the least disposed to grant your request.

And, indeed, to receive you, as you exhibit yourself now, would be a downright act of infidelity: it would not be a renewal with my former lover; it would be taking a new one, many degrees inferior to him. I have not so soon forgot the first, to be deceived. The Valmont I loved was a charming fellow. I will even own, I never met a more amiable man. I beg, Viscount, if you find him, to bring him to me, he will be always well received.

Acquaint him, however, that it cannot by any means be either to-day or to-morrow. His Menæchmus has done him some harm, and was I in too much haste, I should dread a deception; or, perhaps, I have given my word to Danceny for those two days: moreover, your letter informs me you do not jest; when one breaks their word, therefore, you see you must wait.

That is, however, of very little consequence, as you can always be revenged on your rival. He will not treat your mistress worse than you will his; and after all, is not one woman as good as another? These are your own principles. Even she who should be *tender and sensible, who existed only for you, who was dying of love and grief,* would nevertheless be sacrificed to the first whim, or the dread of being ridiculed for a moment; and yet you would have one constrain themselves! Ah! that is not reasonable.

Adieu, Viscount! become once more amiable. It is the utmost of my wishes to find you charming as ever. When I am certain of it, I engage to prove it to you—indeed, I am too good natured.

Paris, Dec. 4, 17—.

LETTER CLIII
VISCOUNT DE VALMONT to the
MARCHIONESS DE MERTEUIL

I reply to your letter on the instant, and will endeavour to be explicit; which is not an easy matter with you, when you have once determined not to understand.

Many words are not necessary to convince us, each has the power of ruining the other; we have an equal interest to keep fair with one another: that is not the business at present. But between the violent determination of destruction, and doubtless the more eligible one of being still united as hitherto, or of even being more so, by renewing our first attachment; between those two parties, I say, there are a thousand more to be taken. It was not, then, ridiculous to tell you, neither is it to repeat, that from this day I will either be your lover or your enemy.

I am very sensible the choice will give you some uneasiness; that it would be more convenient for you to shuffle. I am also satisfied, you never liked to be confined to yes or no: but you must be sensible, I cannot let you from this small circle, without risking being deceived; and you ought to have foreseen, I would not bear it. You are now to decide. I may leave you the choice, but will not remain in uncertainty.

I only inform you beforehand, I will not be imposed on by your arguments, good or bad; that I will no longer be seduced by any ornamental wheedling with which you might embellish a refusal; and that the hour of frankness is arrived. I wish for nothing more than to set you the example; and I declare with pleasure, I prefer peace and union. If it is necessary to break one or the other, I think I have the right and the means.

Therefore I will add, the least obstacle you make, I shall consider as a declaration of war. You will observe, the answer I demand does not require either long or studied sentences: two words will be sufficient.

Paris, Dec. 4, 17—.

The answer of the Marchioness de Merteuil, wrote at the bottom of this same letter.

War, then.

LETTER CLIV
MADAME DE VOLANGES to
MADAME DE ROSEMONDE

The journal will inform you much better than I can, my dear friend, the melancholy state of our patient. Totally employed in my attendance on her, I have scarce time to write to you, as there are other matters to be attended to as well as her disorder. Here is a specimen of one which most certainly I did not in the least expect. I have received a letter from M. de Valmont, who has been pleased to choose me for a confidant, and even his mediatrix with Madame de Tourvel, to whom he wrote under my cover. I returned the one when I answered the other. I transmit you my answer; and I believe you will be of my opinion, that I neither could or ought to have any thing to do with what he requests. Had I been even inclined to it, our unhappy friend was unable to understand me. Her frenzy is incessant. But what do you think of M. de Valmont's distraction? Is it real, or does he mean to deceive the world to the last?[1]

If he is sincere this time, he may well say, he has made himself happy. I believe he will not be well pleased with my answer: but, I own, every thing that fixes my attention on this unhappy adventure, raises my resentment more and more against the author of it.

Adieu, my dear friend! I must return to my melancholy employment, which becomes more so, by the small prospect there is of success. I need not repeat my sentiments for you.

Paris, Dec. 5, 17—.

> [1] Nothing having appeared in this correspondence that could resolve this doubt, we chose to suppress Valmont's letter.

LETTER CLV
The VISCOUNT DE VALMONT to
the CHEVALIER DANCENY

I called on you twice, my dear Chevalier; but since you have thrown off the character of a lover for the man of intrigue, you are very properly invisible: however, your valet assured me you would be at home to-night; that you had ordered him to expect you. I, who am well acquainted with your designs, immediately conjectured it would be but for a short time for fashion's sake, and that you would immediately pursue your victorious career. Go on; I must applaud you: but, perhaps, you will be tempted to alter your course for this night. You are yet acquainted with only half your business; I must let you into the other half, and then you will resolve. Take time, then, to read my letter. It will not dissipate you from your enjoyments; on the contrary, its object is to give you your choice.

If you had opened your mind confidentially to me; if you had told me the part of your secrets you left me to guess at, I should with my zeal, and less awkwardness, have smoothed the path of your progression. But let us set out from this point. Whatever resolution you take would, at worst, be the summit of good fortune to any one else.

You have a rendezvous for to-night: have you not? With a charming woman, whom you adore? For at your age, where is the woman one does not adore for, at least, the first eight days? The field of action should also add greatly to your enjoyment—A delicious little villa, *which was taken for you only*, must embellish voluptuousness with the charms of mysteriousness and liberty. All is agreed on: you are expected; and you are inflamed with desire to be there! All this we both know, though you told me nothing of it. Now I will tell you what you do not know; but you must be told.

Since my return to Paris, I have been taken up with contriving the means of an interview between you and Mademoiselle de Volanges: I promised it; and when I last mentioned it to you, I had reason to expect from your answer, I may say, from your transports, I was exerting myself in your happiness. I could not succeed alone in this difficult undertaking: but after having settled every thing, I left the rest with your young mistress. She found resources in her affection, resources which escaped my experience; after all, to your great misfortune she has succeeded. She told me this evening, for these two days past all obstacles are removed, and your happiness depends on yourself alone.

She flattered herself, also, for those two days, to have been able to send you this news herself, and notwithstanding her mama's absence you would have been admitted: but you never once showed yourself! and I must farther tell you, whether from reason or capriciousness, the little thing did not seem pleased at your want of assiduity. At last she found means to see me, and made me promise to deliver you the enclosed letter as soon as possible. From the eagerness she expressed, I would venture to lay a wager she gives you an assignation this night; however, I promised her, upon honour and friendship, you should have the tender summons in the course of the day, and neither can or will break my word.

Now, young gentleman, how will you behave in this business? Placed between coquetry and love, pleasure and happiness, which will you choose? If I was writing to the Danceny of three months ago, or even the Danceny of a week past, certain of the emotions of his heart, I should be certain of his proceedings: but the Danceny of the day, carried away by women, hunting after intrigue, and, according to custom, a little profligate, will he prefer a timorous young girl, who has nothing but beauty innocence, and love, to the allurements of a common *intriguer?*

For my part, my dear friend, I think, even in your new system, which, I confess, I am not much averse to, circumstances would decide the preference to the lover. First, it is an additional conquest, then the novelty is attracting, and the fear of losing the fruits of your addresses, by neglecting to gather them; for to take it in this point of view, it would really be an opportunity missed, which is not always to be regained, especially in a first weakness: often in this case, a moment of ill humour, a jealous suspicion, even less, may prevent the finest conquest. Sinking virtue will sometimes grasp at a twig; and once escaped, will be on its guard, and not easily surprised.

On the other hand, you hazard nothing; not even a rupture; at most, a little quarrel: then your purchase with a little trouble the pleasure of a reconciliation; for what other resource has a woman you have already enjoyed but compliance? What would she get by severity? The privation of pleasure, without profit, for her glory.

If, as I suppose, you make love your choice, which appears to me, also, that of reason, I think it would be more prudent not to send any apology for the disappointment of the rendezvous; leave her in expectancy; for if you venture to give a reason, she will, perhaps, be tempted to dive into the truth.

Women are curious and obstinate. All may be discovered: I myself, you see, am now an example of this truth. But if you let her remain in hope, which will be supported by vanity, it will not be lost until a long time after the proper hour for information is over; then to-morrow you will have time to choose the insurmountable obstacle that detained you: you may have been sick, dead if necessary, or any thing else that has almost made you frantic, and all will be made up.

But which ever side you incline to, I only beg you will inform me; and as I am totally unconcerned, I will always think you have done right. Adieu, my dear friend!

All I have to add is, I regret M. de Tourvel. I am in a state of desperation at being separated from her; and I would lay down one half my life, to devote the other to her. Ah! believe me, there is no felicity but in love.

Paris, Dec. 5, 17—.

LETTER CLVI
CECILIA VOLANGES to the
CHEVALIER DANCENY

(Annexed to the former.)

How happens it, my dear friend, I no longer see you; although I never cease wishing for it? Your inclinations then, are no longer like mine! Ah, it is now I am truly sorrowful! More so, than when we were totally separate. The affliction I was used to receive from others, now proceeds from you, which is more insupportable.

For some days past, mama is never at home, and you know it—I flattered myself you would have taken the opportunity; but you do not at all think of me—I am very unhappy—How often have you told me, I did not love as much as you did—I was certain it was otherwise, and am now convinced. Had you called, you might have seen me; for I am not like you; I think of nothing but how to contrive to see you—You deserve I should not tell you all I have done: but I love you so much, and have so strong a desire to see you, I can't help telling you, and then I shall see if you really love me.

I have secured the porter, and he has promised every time you come no one shall see you; and we may confide in him, for he is a very honest man. There is then no other difficulty to prevent any one in the house seeing you, and that will be very easy to do; it is only to come at night; then there will be no danger at all—for since mama goes out every day, she always goes to bed at eleven; so that we shall have a great deal of time.

The porter told me when you had a mind to come this way, instead of knocking at the door, you need only tap at the window, and he would open the door directly, and then you can readily find the *back-stairs*—As you will not have any light, I will leave my chamber door open, which will give you some little. You must take great care not to make any noise, particularly passing by mama's little door. As to my waiting maid's room, it is of no signification, for she has promised me not to be awake; and she is also a very good girl! When you are going away it will be the same thing—Now we shall see whether you will come.

O, Lord! I don't know why my heart beats so while I am writing to you! Is it the fore-runner of any misfortune, or is it the hope of seeing you that makes me thus? This I know, I never loved you so much, and never so much wished to tell you so. Come, then, my dear, dear friend, that I may a thousand times repeat I love you—I adore you, and never will love any but you.

I found a method to inform M. de Valmont I wanted to see him, and had something to say to him; and as he is our very good friend, will come to-morrow certainly. I will beg of him to give you my letter immediately—That I shall expect you to-morrow night, and you will not fail to come, if you have not a mind to make your Cecilia very miserable.

Adieu, my dear friend! I embrace you with all my heart.

Paris, Dec. 4, 17—.

LETTER CLVII
The CHEVALIER DANCENY to the VISCOUNT DE VALMONT

Doubt neither the emotions of my heart, or my proceedings, my dear Viscount—Is it possible I could resist a wish of my Cecilia's? Ah! it is she, and she alone, I will ever love! Her openness, her tenderness, have fixed such a spell over me, that nothing can ever efface, although I have been weak enough to suffer a distraction. Imperceptibly, I may say, engaged in another adventure, the remembrance of Cecilia has disturbed me in the tenderest moments; and perhaps my heart never rendered her a more faithful homage, than at the instant I was unfaithful to her. However, my dear friend, let us spare her delicacy, and hide my fault; not to deceive, but only not to afflict her. Cecilia's happiness is the most ardent wish of my heart; and I should never forgive myself a fault which should cost her a tear.

I feel I deserved the banter you pass upon me, relative to what you call my new system: but I beg you will be assured, I am not led by them at this time; I am resolved to prove it to-morrow—I will go and accuse myself even to her who has been the cause and partner of my error—I will tell her; "read my heart; there you will see the tenderest friendship; friendship united to desire so much resembles love! We have both been deceived; but although liable to error, I am incapable of deceit." I know my friend well; she has probity, and is gentle; she will do more than pardon, she will approve my conduct; she has often reproached herself for having betrayed friendship: her delicacy has often alarmed her love: more considerate than me, she will strengthen my mind with those useful apprehensions which I rashly endeavoured to stifle in hers—I shall owe my reformation to her, and my felicity to you. O, my friends! partake my gratitude: the idea of being indebted to you for my happiness, augments its value.

Adieu, my dear Viscount! the excess of my joy does not prevent me from thinking and sharing your troubles. Why can I not serve you? M. de Tourvel still remains inexorable then! It is said she is very ill—May she at once recover health and condescension, and for ever make you happy! They are the vows of friendship; and I dare hope will be granted by love.

I would write some time longer, but time presses, and perhaps Cecilia already expects me.

Paris, Dec. 5, 17—.

LETTER CLVIII
The VISCOUNT DE VALMONT to the MARCHIONESS DE MERTEUIL

Well, Marchioness, how are you after the pleasures of last night? Are you not a little fatigued? You must acknowledge Danceny is a charming fellow! That lad is a prodigy! You did not expect such things from him; is it not true? I must do myself justice; such a rival deserved I should be sacrificed to him. Seriously he has a number of good qualities! So much love, so much constancy, so much delicacy! Ah! if ever he loves you as he does his Cecilia, you will have no occasion to dread being rivalled; he has proved it this night. Perhaps through dint of coquetry, another woman may entice him for a short time; a young man hardly knows how to resist incitements; but you see a single word from the beloved object is sufficient to dissipate the illusion; so that there is nothing wanting to complete your happiness, but being that beloved object.

Certainly you will not be mistaken; you have such exquisite feeling it is not to be apprehended: yet the friendship that unites us, as sincere on my side as acknowledged on yours, made me wish you should experience the proof of this night; it is an effort of my zeal—It has succeeded—But no acknowledgements—it is not worth while—nothing more easy.

But to the point; what did it cost me? Why a slight sacrifice, and a little address. I consented to share with the young man the favours of his mistress; but he had as great a right to them as I had, and I was not in the least uneasy about them. The letter the young creature wrote him, I dictated; but it was only to gain a little time, as we could employ it to so much better purpose. What I wrote with it was nothing, almost nothing. Some few friendly reflections to direct the new lover; but upon honour they were useless—To tell the truth, he did not hesitate a moment. Moreover, he is to wait on you to-day to relate all; and it certainly will give you great pleasure! He will tell you, *read my heart,* so he writes me; and you see that I will settle every thing. I hope that in reading what he pleases, you will also perhaps read, that such young lovers are dangerous—and also, that it is better to have me for a friend than an enemy.

Paris, Dec. 6, 17—.

LETTER CLIX
The MARCHIONESS DE MERTEUIL
to the VISCOUNT DE VALMONT

I do not like to have scurvy jests added to bad actions; it is not agreeable to my taste or manner. When I have cause of complaint against a person, I do not ridicule, I do better; I take revenge. However well pleased you may be with yourself now, do not forget it is not the first time you have applauded yourself beforehand; and singular, in the hope of a triumph that would escape from you, at the instant you was congratulating yourself on it. Adieu.

Paris, Dec. 6, 17—.

LETTER CLX
MADAME DE VOLANGES to
MADAME DE ROSEMONDE

I write this from the chamber of your unhappy friend, whose state is pretty much the same: there is to be a consultation held this afternoon, of four physicians—I need not tell you this resource is oftener a proof of the danger than the means of relief.

However, it seems her head is something better since last night—her waiting maid told me this morning, her mistress ordered her to be called about twelve: she desired they should be left alone, and dictated a pretty long letter—Julie adds, while she was folding it, Madame Tourvel was attacked with her delirium, so that the girl did not know who to direct it to. I was at first surprised the letter itself was not sufficient to inform her; but telling me she was afraid of committing a mistake, and that her mistress had ordered her to send it away immediately, I took it upon me to open it.

There I found the enclosed writing, which is certainly not addressed to any body, being addressed to too many—Yet, I believe, our unhappy friend at first intended it for M. de Valmont, but gave way imperceptibly, to her disordered ideas. However, I thought it ought not to be sent to any one—I send it you, as you will see better than I can tell you, the thoughts that engage the head of our patient. Whilst she continues so intensely affected, I shall have very little hopes—the body seldom recovers when the mind is so agitated.

Adieu, my dear and worthy friend! I am happy you are far from the dismal spectacle I have incessantly before my eyes.

Paris, Dec. 6, 17—.

LETTER CLXI
The Presidente DE TOURVEL

(Dictated by her, and wrote by her waiting maid.)

Cruel and mischievous being! will thou never be tired persecuting me? Is it not enough to have tormented, degraded, abased? Will thou then rob me of the peaceful tomb? In the gloom of this abode, where shame has drove me to bury myself, are my sufferings to have no respite; is hope to be for ever banished? I do not require a favour I am undeserving of: I shall suffer without complaint, if my sufferings do not exceed my strength: but do not make my torments insupportable—Leave me my sorrows, and take away the cruel remembrance of the advantages I have lost. Although thou hast ravished them from me, do not again draw the afflicting picture of them—I was happy and innocent—I gazed on thee and lost my peace—I listened to thee and was guilty—Thou cause of all my crimes, who gave thee authority to punish them?

Where are now the friends to whom I was dear? My misfortunes have frightened them—No one dares come near me—I am oppressed and left without relief—I die and no one weeps over me—I am debarred of every consolation—Pity stops on the brink of the abyss where the criminal plunges—remorse tears my heart, and its cries are not heard.

And thou who I have injured; thou, whose esteem adds to my torment—thou who only hast a right to revenge; why art thou far from me? Come, punish a faithless woman—Let me suffer the tortures I deserve—I should have already bowed to thy vengeance, but wanted courage to inform thee of thy shame; it was not dissimulation, it was respect. Let this letter at least acquaint thee with my repentance. Heaven has taken thy cause in hand, to punish an injury to which thou wast a stranger—It was heaven tied my tongue—It was heaven prevented my design, lest you should pardon a crime it was resolved to punish—It snatched me from thy commiseration, which would have opposed its judgment.

But unmerciful in its vengeance, it delivered me up to him who ruined me; at once to make me suffer for him and by him. In vain I strive to fly from him; still he follows me—he is there; incessantly he besets me—How different from himself! His eyes show nothing but hatred and contempt—

His lips utter insult and reproach—His arms surround me only to destroy me—Is there no one will save me from his savage rage?

How! It is he! I am not deceiv'd; it is he I see again—Oh, my lovely friend! receive me in thy tender arms; hide me in thy bosom! It is thee; yes, it is thyself—What fatal illusion deceived me? Ah, how have I suffered during thy absence—Let us part no more: let us never part. Let me breathe—Feel my heart, how it beats! Ah! it is no longer with fear, it is the soft emotion of love; why refuse my tender caresses? Turn thy languishing eyes towards me— What are those bands you want to break? Why those solemn preparations for death? What can thus alter thy countenance? Leave me! I shudder! O, God! This monster again! My dear friends, do not abandon me—You that wanted me to avoid him; help me to resist him—And you more lenient, who promised to soften my sorrows, why do not you come to me? Where are you both? If I must no longer see you, at least answer this letter, let me hear you still love me.

Leave me, then, cruel man! What new transport inspires thee? Art thou afraid a soft sentiment should invade me? thou redoublest my torments— You will force me to hate you—O, how painful is hatred! how it corrodes the heart from whence it is distilled! Why will you persecute me? What can you have more to say to me? Have you not made it impossible for me either to hear or answer you. Farewell.

Paris, Dec. 6, 17—.

LETTER CLXII
CHEVALIER DANCENY to the
VISCOUNT DE VALMONT

I am informed, Sir, of your behaviour towards me—I also know that after having basely sported with me, you have dared to applaud yourself and brag of it—The proof of your treachery I have seen under your hand—I cannot help acknowledging my heart was pierced, and I felt some shame at having myself so much assisted in the odious abuse you made of my blind confidence: still I do not envy you this shameful advantage—I am only curious to know, whether you will equally preserve them all over me—This I shall be informed of, if, as I hope, you will be to-morrow morning, between eight and nine, at the gate of the wood of Vincennes, village of St. Maude. I will take care to provide every thing necessary for the eclaircissement, which remains for me to take with you.

The Chevalier Danceny.
Paris, Dec. 6, at night, 17—.

LETTER CLXIII
M. BERTRAND to MADAME DE ROSEMONDE

Madam,

It is with the greatest grief I find myself obliged to fulfil my duty, by giving you an intelligence that will cause you so much affliction. Permit me first to recommend the exertion of that pious resignation which every one has so often admired in you, and which alone can support us among the evils of this miserable life.

M. your nephew—Good God! must I afflict so respectable a lady! M. your nephew, had the misfortune to fall this morning in a duel he fought with M. the Chevalier Danceny. I am entirely unacquainted with the cause of the quarrel: but it appears, by the note which I found in M. the Viscount's pocket, and which I have the honour to send you; it appears, I say, he was not the aggressor: and yet heaven permitted him to fall!

I was at M. the Viscount's, waiting for him, at the very time he was brought back to his hotel. You cannot conceive the shock I received, seeing M. your nephew brought in by two of his servants, bathed in blood. He had two thrusts of a sword in his body, and was very weak. M. Danceny was also there, and even wept. Ah! certainly he ought to weep—it is a pretty time to cry when one has been the cause of an irreparable misfortune!

For my part, I could not contain myself; and notwithstanding my insignificancy, I could not help telling him my thoughts. But it was then M. the Viscount showed himself truly great: he commanded me to hold my tongue; and he even took his murderer by the hand, called him his friend, embraced him before us three, and said to us, "I command you to have for this gentleman all the respect that is due to a brave and gallant man." Moreover, he ordered to be given him, in my presence, some very voluminous papers, that I know nothing of, but which I know he set a value on. Then he desired they should be left together for a little while; however, I sent immediately for assistance, as well spiritual as temporal: but, alas! the evil was without remedy. In less than half an hour after, M. the Viscount was insensible. He could only receive the extreme unction; and the ceremony was scarcely over, before he breathed his last.

Great God! when I received in my arms at his birth this precious prop of so illustrious a family, could I ever have thought he would expire in my arms, and that I should deplore his death! A death so sudden, and so unfortunate—my tears flow in spite of me. I ask pardon, Madam, for taking the liberty of mingling my sorrows with yours: but in every station, tenderness and sensibility will operate; and I should be very ungrateful if I did not lament, during my life, a nobleman who was so kind, and placed such a confidence in me.

To-morrow, when the body will be removed, I will order every thing to be sealed, and you may depend on my care entirely in every thing. I need not inform you, Madam, this unhappy event puts an end to the entail, and leaves you entirely at liberty. If I can be of any service, I beg, Madam, you will give me your orders, which will be executed with the greatest zeal and utmost punctuality.

I am, with the most profound respect, Madam, your most humble Bertrand.

Paris, Dec. 7, 17—.

LETTER CLXIV
MADAME DE ROSEMONDE to M. BERTRAND

I this instant received your letter, my dear Bertrand, informing me of the shocking event, to which my nephew is become the unhappy victim—yes, undoubtedly, I shall have orders to give you; and it is they only can take off my thoughts a while from this afflicting intelligence.

M. Danceny's challenge, which you sent me, is a convincing proof he was the aggressor; my intention therefore is, you should commence a prosecution in my name: for although my nephew, in compliance with his natural generosity, may have pardoned his enemy, his murderer, I ought to avenge at once his death, religion, and humanity. One cannot excite too much the severity of the laws against those remains of barbarism which still infect our morals; and I do not believe, in such cases, the forgiveness of injuries can be commanded us; therefore I expect you will prosecute this business with all that zeal and activity of which I know you so capable, and which you owe to my nephew's memory.

But first, take care to confer with M. the President — — from me. I do not write to him, as I am so overwhelmed with grief. You will, therefore, apologise for me, and communicate this to him.

Adieu, my dear Bertrand! I am well pleased with your conduct, and thank you for your good inclinations, and am your sincere friend.

Castle of — —, Dec. 8, 17—.

LETTER CLXV
MADAME DE VOLANGES to
MADAME DE ROSEMONDE

I know you are already informed, my dear and worthy friend, of the loss you have sustained. I know the tender affection you had for M. de Valmont, and I most sincerely partake of the affliction you must endure. I am truly grieved to add new griefs to those you have already experienced: but, alas! nothing now can be done for our unhappy friend but to deplore her fate. We lost her at eleven o'clock last night. By a fatality linked to her fate, and which seemed to baffle all human prudence, this short interval that she survived M. de Valmont was sufficient to inform her of his death, and, as she said herself, not be able to sink under the weight of her miseries until their measure was filled.

You already know, that for these two days she was insensible;—yesterday morning, when her physician came, and we drew near her bed, she did not know either of us, and we could not obtain a word or a sign. We were scarcely returned to the fire, while the physician was relating to me the melancholy event of M. de Valmont's death, but this unhappy woman recovered her reason: whether nature alone produced this revolution, or whether it was occasioned by the frequent repetition of the words, M. de Valmont and death, which may have recalled the only ideas with which her mind had been so long engaged.

Be it what it may, she suddenly drew back the curtain of the bed, exclaiming, "What! What do you say? M. de Valmont dead!" I hoped to make her believe she was mistaken. At first I endeavoured to persuade her she did not hear well: but all in vain; for she insisted the physician should begin the cruel tale again;—on my endeavouring to dissuade her from it, she called me to her, saying, in a low voice, "Why will you deceive me? Was he not already dead to me?" I then was forced to acquiesce.

Our unhappy friend appeared at first to listen to the story with great tranquillity: but she soon interrupted him, saying, "Enough; I know enough:" and immediately ordered her curtains to be closed—When the physician went to perform the duties of his office, she never would suffer him to come near her.

As soon as he was gone, she also sent away her nurse and her waiting maid. When we were alone, she requested I would assist her to kneel on her bed, and support her. Then she remained some time silent;—and without any other expression than her tears, which flowed most abundantly, joining her hands, and raising them towards heaven; "Almighty God!" said she in a weak but fervent tone, "I submit to thy just judgment: but in thy mercy forgive Valmont. Let not my misfortunes, which I acknowledge, be laid to his charge, and I shall bless thy mercy!" I could not avoid, my dear and worthy friend, going into those digressions on a subject I am sensible must renew and aggravate your sorrows, as I am certain this prayer of Madame de Tourvel's will give you much consolation.

After our friend had uttered those few words she fell in my arms; and she was scarcely settled in her bed, when she fainted for a considerable time, and recovered with the usual helps. As soon as she came to herself, she begged I would send for Father Anselmus, saying, "He is the only physician I have now occasion for. I feel my miseries will soon be at end." She complained of a great oppression, and spoke with great difficulty.

Some time after, she ordered her waiting maid to give me a little box, which I send you, that contains papers belonging to her, and charged me to send them to you immediately after her death.[1] Then she conversed about you, of your friendship for her, as much as her situation would permit, and with great tenderness.

Father Anselmus came about four o'clock, and stayed near an hour alone with her. When we returned, her countenance was calm and serene, but it was easily to be seen Father Anselmus had wept a great deal. He remained to assist at the last ceremonies of the church. This solemn and melancholy sight became more so by the contrast of the composed and settled resignation of the sick person, with the silent grief of the venerable confessor, who was dissolved in tears beside her. The afflicting scene became general, and she who we all deplored was the only one unmoved.

The remainder of the day was spent in the usual prayers, which was now and then interrupted by the frequent faintings of the dear woman. At last, about eleven, she seemed more in pain, with great oppression. I put out my hand to feel her arm; she had still strength to place it on her heart; I could no longer feel it beat, and, indeed, our unhappy friend expired instantly.

You may remember, my dear friend, when you last came to town, about a year ago, chatting together about some people whose happiness then appeared to us more or less complete, we indulged ourselves in the thought of this same woman's felicity, whose misfortune we now lament. Such an assemblage of virtues! so many attractions and accomplishments! so sweet, so amiable! a husband she loved, and by whom she was adored! a circle of friends, in whom she delighted, and was the delight! a figure, youth, fortune! so many united advantages are lost by one act of imprudence! O, Providence! how incomprehensible and adorable are thy decrees!—I fear I shall increase your sorrow by giving way to my own, and therefore will no longer dwell on the melancholy theme.

My daughter is a little indisposed. On hearing from me this morning the sudden death of two persons of her acquaintance, she was taken ill, and I ordered her to be put to bed. I hope, however, this slight disorder will not be attended with any bad consequence. At her age they are not accustomed to such chagrines, and they leave a more lively and stronger impression. This active sensibility is certainly a laudable quality. What we daily see ought to make us dread it. Adieu, my dear and worthy friend!

Paris, Dec. 9, 17—.

[1] This box contained all the letters relative to her adventure with M. de Valmont.

LETTER CLXVI
M. BERTRAND to MADAME DE ROSEMONDE

Madam,

In consequence of the orders you honoured me with, I waited on M. the President de — —, and communicated your letter to him, informing him at the same time, as you desired, I should do nothing without his advice. This respectable magistrate commanded me to observe to you, the prosecution you intended against M. the Chevalier Danceny would equally affect the memory of Monsieur your nephew, and his honour would necessarily be tainted by the decree of the court; which would be, doubtless, a very great misfortune. His opinion is, then, that you do not make any stir about the matter: but, on the contrary, that you should endeavour as much as possible to prevent the public officers from taking cognisance of this unfortunate business, which has already made too much noise.

These observations, so replete with wisdom, oblige me to wait your farther orders.

Permit me, Madam, to request, when you honour me with them, you will mention a word concerning your state of health, which, I dread much, so many crosses have impaired.

I hope you will pardon the liberty I take, as it proceeds from my zeal and attachment.

I am, with great respect, Madam, your, &c.
Paris, Dec. 10, 17—.

LETTER CLXVII
ANONYMOUS to the CHEVALIER DANCENY

Sir,

I have the honour to inform you, your late affair with M. the Viscount de Valmont was this morning much talked of among the King's counsel within the bar, and that it is much to be feared the public officers will commence a prosecution. I thought this notice might be of service, either to set your friends at work, to stop the bad consequences, or, in case you could not succeed, to take every precaution for your personal security.

If you would permit me to add a piece of advice, I think you would do well, for some time at least, not to appear so much in public as you have done for some days—Although the world generally have great indulgence for those kind of affairs, yet there is a respect due to the laws which ought to be observed.

This precaution appears to me the more necessary, that I recollect a Madame de Rosemonde, who, I am told, is M. de Valmont's aunt, intended to prosecute you; if so, the courts could not refuse her petition: it would perhaps be proper application should be made to this lady.

Particular reasons prevent me from signing this letter; but I hope, though ignorant from whom it comes, you will nevertheless do justice to the sentiment that has dictated it.

I have the honour to be, &c.
Paris, Dec. 10, 17—.

LETTER CLXVIII
MADAME DE VOLANGES to
MADAME DE ROSEMONDE

There are, my dear and worthy friend, the strangest and most sad reports spread here, on account of Madam de Merteuil. I am certainly far from giving any credit to them; and I would venture to lay a wager, they are horrible slanders; but I know too well, how the most improbable wickedness readily gains credit; and how difficult it is to wipe away the impression they leave, not to be alarmed at those, though I think them so easy to be refuted. I wish, especially, they might be stopped in time, and before they spread abroad; but I did not know until late yesterday, the horrible things that are given out; and when I sent this morning to Madame de Merteuil's, she was just then set out for the country for a couple of days—I could not learn where she was gone; her second woman, who I sent for, told me, her mistress had only given her orders to expect her on Thursday next; and none of her servants she left behind her knew any thing. I cannot even think where she can be; as I do not recollect any of her acquaintance who stay so late in the country.

However, you will be able, I hope, to procure for me, between this and her return, some eclaircissements that may be useful to her; for these odious stories are founded on circumstances attendant on the death of M. de Valmont, of which you will probably have been informed, if there be any truth in them; or you can at least readily receive information, which I particularly request you to do—This is what is published, or at least whispered as yet, but will not certainly fail to blaze out more.

It is said the quarrel between M. de Valmont and Chevalier Danceny, is the work of Madame de Merteuil, who deceived them both; and, as it always happens, the rivals began by fighting, and did not come to an eclaircissement until after, which produced a sincere reconciliation: and in order to make M. de Merteuil known to Chevalier Danceny, and also in his own justification, M. de Valmont had added to his intelligence, a heap of letters, forming a regular correspondence which he had kept up with her; in which she relates, in the loosest manner, the most scandalous anecdotes of herself.

It is added, that Danceny in his first rage gave those letters to whoever had a mind to see them; and that now they are all over Paris—Two of them in particular, are quoted[1]; in one of which, she gives a full history of her life and principles, which are said to be the most shocking imaginable—the other contains an entire justification of M. de Prevan, whose story you may recollect, by the proofs it gives, that he did nothing but acquiesce in the most pointed advances M. de Merteuil made him, and the rendezvous agreed on with her.

But I have fortunately the strongest reasons to believe those imputations as false as they are odious. First, we both know that M. de Valmont was not engaged about Madame de Merteuil; and I have all the reason in the world to think, Danceny was as far from thinking of her: so that I think it is demonstrable, that she could not be either the cause or object of the quarrel. Neither can I comprehend what interest M. de Merteuil could have, who is supposed to be combined with M. de Prevan, to act a part which must be very disagreeable, by the noise it would occasion, and might be very dangerous for her, because she would thereby make an irreconcileable enemy of a man who was in possession of a part of her secrets, and who had then many partizans.—Still it is observable, since that adventure, not a single voice has been raised in favour of Prevan, and that even there has not been the least objection made on his side since.

Those reflections would induce me to suspect him to be the author of the reports that are now spread abroad, and to look on those enormities as the work of the revenge and hatred of a man who, finding himself lost in the opinion of the world, hopes, by such means, at least to raise doubts, and perhaps make a useful diversion in his favour; but whatever cause they may proceed from, the best way will be to destroy such abominable tales as soon as possible; they would have dropped of themselves, if it should happen, as is very probable, that M. de Valmont and Danceny did not speak to each other after their unhappy affair, and that there had been no papers given.

Being impatient to be satisfied as to the truth of those facts, I sent this morning to M, Danceny's; he is not in Paris either; his servants told my valet de chambre, he had set out last night, on some advice he had received yesterday, and the place of his residence was a secret; probably he dreads the consequence of his affair; it is only from you then, my dear and worthy friend, I can learn such interesting particulars, that may be necessary for M. de Merteuil—I renew my request, and beg you will send them to me as soon as possible.

P. S. My daughter's indisposition had no bad consequences. She presents her respects.

Paris, Dec. 11, 17—.

[1] Letters lxxxi and lxxxv.

LETTER CLXIX
The CHEVALIER DANCENY to MADAME DE ROSEMONDE

Madam,

You will perhaps think the step I now take very extraordinary; but I beseech you to hear before you condemn me, and do not look for either audacity or rashness, where there is nothing but respect and confidence. I will not dissemble the injury I have done you; and during my whole life I should never forgive myself, if I could for one moment think it had been possible for me to avoid it; I also beg, Madam, you will be persuaded, although I feel myself exempt from reproach, I am not exempt from sorrow; and I can with the greatest sincerity add, those I have caused you have a great share in those I feel. To believe in those sentiments which I now presume to assure you of, it will be enough you do yourself justice, and know, that without the honour of being known to you, yet I have that of knowing you.

Still whilst I lament the fatality which has caused at once your grief and my misfortune, I am taught to believe, that totally taken up with a thirst for revenge, you sought means to satiate it even in the severity of the laws.

Permit me first to observe on this subject, that here your grief deceives you; for my interest in this circumstance is so intimately linked with M. de Valmont's, that his memory would be involved in the same sentence you would have excited against me. I should then reasonably suppose, Madam, I should rather expect assistance than obstacles from you, in the endeavours I should be obliged to make, that this unhappy event should remain buried in oblivion.

But this resource of complicity, which is equally favourable to the innocent and guilty, is not sufficient to satisfy my delicacy; in wishing to set you aside as a party, I call on you as my judge: the esteem of those I respect is too dear, to suffer me to lose yours without defending it, and I think I am furnished with the means.

For if you will only agree, that revenge is permitted, or rather, that a man owes it to himself, when he is betrayed in his love, in his friendship, and still more, in his confidence. If you agree to this, the wrongs I have done will disappear: I do not ask you to believe what I say; but read, if you have the resolution, the deposit I put into your hands[1]; the number of original letters seem to authenticate those, of which there is only copies. Moreover, I received those letters, as I have the honour to transmit them to you, from M. de Valmont himself. I have not added to them, nor have I taken any from them but two letters, which I thought proper to publish.

The one was necessary to the mutual vengeance of M. de Valmont and myself, to which we had an equal right, and of which he expressly gave me a charge. I moreover thought, it would be doing an essential service to society, to unmask a woman so really dangerous as Madame de Merteuil is, and who, as you see, is the only, the true cause, of what happened between M. de Valmont and me.

A sentiment of justice induced me to publish the second, for the justification of M. de Prevan, whom I scarcely know; but who did not in the least deserve the rigorous treatment he has met, nor the severity of the public opinion, still more formidable, under which he has languished so long, without being able to make any defence.

You will only find copies of those two letters, as I make it a point to keep the originals. I do not think I can put into safer hands a deposit, which, perhaps, I think of consequence to me not to be destroyed, but which I should be ashamed to abuse. I think, confiding those papers to you, Madam, I serve those who are interested, as well as if I returned them to themselves, and I preserve them from the embarrassment of receiving them from me, and of knowing I am no stranger to events, which undoubtedly they wish all the world to be unacquainted with.

I should, however, inform you, the annexed correspondence is only a part of a much more voluminous collection from which M. de Valmont drew it in my presence, and which you will find at the taking off the seals, entitled as I saw, *An open account between the Marchioness de Merteuil and Viscount de Valmont*. On this you will take what measures your prudence will suggest. I am with great respect,

Madam, &c.

P. S. Some advices I have received, and the opinion of some friends, have made me resolve to leave Paris for some time; but the place of my retreat, which is secret to every one, must not be so to you. If you do me the honour of an answer, I beg you will direct it to the commandery of — — by

P.—and under cover, to M. the Commander of ——. It is from his house I have the honour to write to you.

Paris, Dec. 12, 17—.

[1] It is from this correspondence, from that given at the death of M. de Tourvel, and the letters confided to M. Rosemonde, by Madame de Volanges, that the present collection has been compiled; the originals are still existing in the possession of Madame de Rosemonde's heirs.

LETTER CLXX
MADAME DE VOLANGES to
MADAME DE ROSEMONDE

I go, my dear friend, from wonder to wonder, from sorrow to sorrow: one must be a mother to conceive my sufferings all yesterday morning—If my cruel uneasiness has been since alleviated, there still remains a piercing affliction, of which I cannot see the end.

Yesterday, about ten in the morning, surprised at not seeing my daughter, I sent my waiting maid to know what could occasion this delay— She returned instantly much frightened, and frightened me much more, by telling me my daughter was not in her apartment, and that since morning her waiting maid had not seen her. Judge you my situation! I had all my servants called, particularly the porter, who all swore they knew nothing of her, nor gave me any intelligence on this occasion. I went immediately into her apartment; the disorder it was in soon convinced me, she did not go out until morning, but could not discover any thing to clear up my doubts. I examined her drawers, her bureau; found every thing in its place, and all her clothes except the dress she had on when she went out: she did not even take the little money she had.

As she did not know until yesterday all that is said about M. de Merteuil; that she is very much attached to her; so much, that she did nothing but cry all night after—I also recollect she did not know M. de Merteuil was in the country; it struck me she went to see her friend, and that she was so foolish as to go alone: but the time elapsing, and no account of her, recalled all my uneasiness—Every instant increased my anxiety; and burning with impatience for information, I dared not take any step to be informed, lest I should give cause for a rumour, which perhaps I should afterwards wish to hide from all the world. In my life I never suffered so much.

At length, at past two o'clock, I received together a letter from my daughter, and one from the superior of the convent of ——. My daughter's letter only informed me, she was afraid I would oppose the vocation she had to a religious life, which she did not dare mention to me; the rest was only excusing herself for having taken this resolution without my leave, being assured I certainly would not disapprove it, if I knew her motives, which, however, she begged I would not enquire into.

The superior informed me, that seeing a young person come alone, she at first refused to receive her; but having interrogated, and learning who she was, she thought she served me, by giving an asylum to my daughter, not to expose her to run about, which she certainly was determined on doing. The superior offered me, as was reasonable, to give up my daughter, if I required it; inviting me at the same time, not to oppose a vocation she calls so decided.

She writes me also, she could not inform me sooner of this event, by the difficulty she had of prevailing on my daughter to write to me whose intent was, that no one should know where she had retired — What a cruel thing is the unreasonableness of children.

I went immediately to this convent. After having seen the superior, I desired to see my daughter; she came trembling, with some difficulty — I spoke to her before the nuns, and then alone. All I could get out of her with a deal of crying, was, she could not be happy but in a convent; I resolved to give her leave to stay there; but not to be ranked among those who desired admittance as she wanted. I fear M. de Tourvel's and M. de Valmont's deaths have too much affected her young head. Although I respect much a religious vocation, I shall not without sorrow, and even dread, see my daughter embrace this state — I think we have already duties enough to fulfil, without creating ourselves new ones: moreover, it is not at her age we can judge what condition is suitable for us.

What increases my embarrassment, is the speedy return of M. de Gercourt — Must I break off this advantageous match? How then can one contribute to their children's happiness, if our wishes and cares are not sufficient? You would much oblige me to let me know how you would act in my situation; I cannot fix on any thing. There is nothing so dreadful as to decide on the fate of others; and I am equally afraid, on this occasion, of using the severity of a judge, or the weakness of a mother.

I always reproach myself with increasing your griefs, by relating mine; but I know your heart; the consolation you could give others, would be the greatest you could possibly receive.

Adieu, my dear and worthy friend! I expect your two answers with the greatest impatience.

Paris, Dec. 13, 17—.

LETTER CLXXI
MADAME DE ROSEMONDE to
the CHEVALIER DANCENY

The information you have given me, Sir, leaves me no room for any thing but sorrow and silence. One regrets to live, when they hear such horrible actions; one must be ashamed of their sex, when they see a woman capable of such abominations.

I will willingly assist all in my power, Sir, as far as I am concerned, to bury in silence and forgetfulness every thing that could leave any trace or consequence to those melancholy events. I even wish they may never give you any other uneasiness than those inseparable from the unhappy advantage you gained over my nephew. Notwithstanding his faults, which I am forced to confess, I feel I shall never be consoled for his loss: but my everlasting affliction will be the only revenge I shall ever take on you; I leave it to your own heart to value its extent.

Will you permit my age to make a reflection which seldom occurs to yours? which is, if rightly understood what is solid happiness, we should never seek it beyond the bounds prescribed by religion and the laws.

You may be very certain I will faithfully and willingly keep the deposit you have confided to me: but I must require of you to authorise me not to deliver it to any one, not even to yourself, Sir, unless it should be necessary for your justification. I dare believe you will not refuse me this request, and that it is now unnecessary to make you sensible we often sigh for having given way to the most just revenge.

I have not yet done with my requisitions, persuaded as I am of your generosity and delicacy: it would be an act worthy both, to give me up also Mademoiselle de Volanges's letters, which you probably may have preserved, and which, no doubt, are no longer interesting. I know this young creature has used you badly; but I do not think you mean to punish her; and was it only out of respect to yourself, you will not debase an object you loved so much. I have, therefore, no occasion to add, the respect the girl is unworthy of, is well due to the mother, to that respectable woman, who may lay some claim to a reparation from you; for, indeed, whatever colour one may seek to put on a pretended sentimental delicacy, he who first attempts to seduce a virtuous and innocent heart, by that measure becomes the first abettor of its corruption, and should be for ever accountable for the excesses and disorders that are the consequence.

Do not be surprised, Sir, at so much severity from me; it is the strongest proof I can give you of my perfect esteem. You will still acquire an additional right to it, if you acquiesce, as I wish, to the concealing a secret, the publication of which would prejudice yourself, and give a mortal stab to a maternal heart you have already wounded. In a word, Sir, I wish to render this service to my friend; and if I had the least apprehension you would refuse me this consolation, I would desire you to think first, it is the only one you had left me.

I have the honour to be, &c.
Castle of — —, Dec. 15, 17—.

LETTER CLXXII
MADAME DE ROSEMONDE to MADAME DE VOLANGES

If I had been obliged to send to Paris, my dear friend, and wait for an answer to the eclaircissements you require concerning Madame de Merteuil, it would not have been possible to give them to you yet; and even then they would be, doubtless, vague and uncertain: but I received some I did not expect, that I had not the least reason to expect, and they are indubitable. O, my dear friend! how greatly you have been deceived in this woman!

I have great reluctance to enter into the particulars of this heap of shocking abominations; but let what will be given out, be assured it will not exceed the truth. I think, my dear friend, you know me sufficiently to take my word, and that you will not require from me any proof. Let it suffice to tell you, there is a multitude of them, which I have now in my possession.

It is not without the greatest trouble I must also make you the same request, not to oblige me to give my motives for the advice you require concerning Mademoiselle de Volanges. I entreat you not to oppose the vocation she shows.

Certainly, no reason whatever should authorise the forcing a person into that state, when there is no call: but it is sometimes a great happiness when there is; and you see your daughter even tells you, if you knew her motives you would not disapprove them. He who inspires us with sentiments, knows better than our vain wisdom can direct, what is suitable to every one; and what is often taken for an act of severity, is an act of his clemency.

Upon the whole, my advice, which I know will afflict you, for which reason you must believe I have reflected well on it, is, that you should leave Mademoiselle de Volanges in the convent, since it is her choice; and that you should rather encourage than counteract the project she has formed; and in expectation of its being put in execution, not to hesitate in breaking off the intended match.

Now that I have fulfilled those painful duties of friendship, and incapable as I am of adding any consolation, the only favour I have to request, my dear friend, is, not to put me any interrogatories on any subject relative to those melancholy events: let us leave them in the oblivion suitable to them; and without seeking useless or afflicting knowledge, submit to the decrees of Providence, confiding in the wisdom of its views whenever it does not permit us to comprehend them. Adieu, my dear friend!

Castle of — —, Dec. 15, 17—.

LETTER CLXXIII
MADAME DE VOLANGES to MADAME DE ROSEMONDE

Alas, my dear friend! with what a frightful veil do you cover the fate of my daughter; and seem to dread I should raise it! What can it hide, then, more afflicting to a mother's heart, than those horrible suspicions to which you give me up? The more I consider your friendship, your indulgence, the more my torments are increased. Twenty times since last night, I wanted to be rid of those cruel uncertainties, and to beg you would inform me, without reserve or evasion, and each time shuddered, when I recollected your request not to be interrogated. At length, I have thought on a way which still gives me some hope; and I expect from your friendship, you will not refuse to grant my wish: which is, to inform me if I have nearly understood what you might have to tell me; not to be afraid to acquaint me with all a mother's tenderness can hide, and is not impossible to be repaired. If my miseries exceed those bounds, then I consent to leave the explanation to your silence: here is, then, what I already know, and so far my fears extended.

My daughter showed a liking for Chevalier Danceny, and I was informed, she went so far as to receive letters from him, and even to answer them; but I thought I had prevented this juvenile error from having any dangerous consequence: now that I am in dread of every thing, I conceive it possible my vigilance may have been deceived, and I dread my daughter being seduced may have completed the measure of her follies.

I now recall to mind several circumstances that may strengthen this apprehension. I wrote you, my daughter was taken ill, on the news of M. de Valmont's misfortune; perhaps, the cause of this sensibility was the idea of the dangers M. Danceny was exposed to in this combat. Since when, she wept so much on hearing every thing was said of Madame de Merteuil; perhaps, what I imagined the grief of friendship, was nothing else but the effect of jealousy, or regret at finding her lover faithless. Her last step may, I think, perhaps be explained by the same motive. Some, who have been disgusted with mankind, have imagined they received a call from heaven. In short, supposing those things to be so, and that you are acquainted with them, you may, no doubt, have thought them sufficient to justify the rigorous advice you give me.

And if matters should be so, at the same time I should blame my daughter, I should think myself bound to attempt every method to save her from the torments and dangers of an illusory and transitory vocation. If M. Danceny is not totally divested of every honourable sentiment, he will not surely refuse to repair an injury of which he is the sole author; and I also think, a marriage with my daughter, not to mention her family, would be advantageously flattering to him.

This, my dear and worthy friend, is my last hope; hasten to confirm it, if possible. You may judge how impatient I shall be for an answer, and what a mortal blow your silence would give me.[1]

I was just closing my letter, when a man of my acquaintance came to see me, and related to me a cruel scene Madame de Merteuil had to go through yesterday. As I saw no one for some days, I heard nothing of this affair. I will recite it, as I had it from an eye witness.

Madame de Merteuil, at her return from the country on Thursday, was set down at the Italian comedy, where she had a box; there she was alone; and what must appear to her very extraordinary, not a man came near her during the whole performance. At coming away, she went, according to custom, into the little saloon, which was full of company; instantly a buzzing began, of which probably she did not think herself the object. She observed an empty place on one of the seats, on which she sat down; but all the ladies who were seated on it immediately rose, as if in concert, and left her entirely alone. This so pointed mark of general indignation was applauded by all the men, redoubled the murmurs, which, it is said, were even at last increased to hootings.

That nothing should be wanting to complete her humiliation, unfortunately for her, M. de Prevan, who had not appeared in public since his adventure, made his appearance at that instant. The moment he entered, every one, men and women, surrounded and applauded him; and he was jostled in such a manner, as to be brought directly opposite M. de Merteuil by the company who formed a circle round him. It is asserted, she preserved the appearance of neither seeing or hearing any thing, and that she did not even change countenance; but I am apt to believe this last an exaggeration. However, this truly ignominious situation lasted until her carriage was announced; and at her departure, those scandalous hootings and hissings were again redoubled. It is shocking to be related to this woman. M. de

Prevan received a most hearty welcome from all the officers of his corps who were there, and there is not the least doubt but he will be restored soon to his rank.

The same person who gave me this information told me M. de Merteuil was taken the night following with a very violent fever, that was at first imagined to be the effect of the dreadful situation she was in; but last night the small pox declared itself, it is of the confluent kind, and of the worst sort. On my word, I think it would be the greatest happiness if it should carry her off. It is, moreover, reported, this affair will prejudice her most essentially in her depending lawsuit, which is soon to be brought to trial, and in which, it is said, she stood in need of powerful protection.

Adieu, my dear and worthy friend! In all this I see the hand of Providence punishing the wicked: but do not find any consolation for their unhappy victims.

Paris, Dec. 18, 17—.

[1] This letter remained unanswered.

LETTER CLXXIV
The CHEVALIER DANCENY to
MADAME DE ROSEMONDE

You are very right, Madam; most certainly I will not refuse you any thing that depends on me, and on which you are inclined to set a value. The packet I have the honour to send you, contains all Mademoiselle de Volanges' letters. If you will take the trouble to read them, you will be astonished to see so much candour united with such perfidiousness. This is, at least, what has made the strongest impression on my mind, at my last perusal of them.

But it is impossible to avoid being filled with the greatest indignation against M. de Merteuil, when one recollects what horrible pleasure and pains she took to destroy so much innocence and candour.

No, Madam, I am no longer in love. I have not the least spark of a sentiment so unworthily betrayed; and it is not love that puts me on means to justify Mademoiselle de Volanges. Still would not that innocent heart, that soft and easy temper, be moulded to good more readily than it was hurried to evil? What young person, just come out of a convent, without experience, and almost divested of ideas, and bringing with her into the world, as most always happens, an equal share of ignorance of good and evil; what young person could have resisted such culpable artifices more? In order to inspire us with some indulgence, it is sufficient to reflect on how many circumstances, independent of us, is the frightful alternative from delicacy, to the depravity of sentiment. You, then, did me justice, Madam, in believing me incapable of having any idea of revenge, for the injuries I received from Mademoiselle de Volanges, and which, notwithstanding, I felt very sensibly. The sacrifice is great, in being obliged to give over loving her: but the attempt would be too great for me to hate her.

I had no need of reflection to wish every thing that concerns, or that could be prejudicial to her, should ever be kept secret from the world. If I have appeared something dilatory in fulfilling your wishes on this occasion, I believe I may tell you my motive; I wished first to be certain I should not be troubled on my late unhappy affair. At a time when I was soliciting your indulgence, when I even dared to think I had some right to it, I should have dreaded having the least appearance in a manner of purchasing it by this condescension: certain of the purity of my motives, I had, I own, the vanity to wish you could not have the least doubt of them.

I hope you will pardon this delicacy, perhaps too susceptible, to the veneration with which you have inspired me, and to the great value of your esteem.

The same sentiment makes me request as a favour, you will be so obliging to let me know if you think I have fulfilled all the obligations the unhappy circumstances I was in required. Once satisfied on this point, my resolution is taken; I set out for Malta: there I shall with pleasure take and religiously keep vows which will separate me from a world, with which, though young, I have so much reason to be dissatisfied—I will endeavour in a foreign clime, to lose the idea of so many accumulated horrors, whose remembrance can only bring sorrow to my head.

I am with the greatest respect, Madam, &c.
Paris, Dec. 26, 17—.

LETTER CLXXV
MADAME DE VOLANGES to
MADAME DE ROSEMONDE

At length, my dear and worthy friend, Madame de Merteuil's fate is determined; and it is such, that her greatest enemies are divided between the indignation she deserves, and the compassion she raises. I was right, when I wrote you it would be happy for her to have died of the small pox. She is recovered, it is true, but horribly disfigured; and has lost an eye. You may well imagine, I have not seen her; but I have been informed she is a hideous spectacle.

The Marquis of — — who never loses an opportunity of saying a sarcastical thing, speaking of her yesterday, said, that her disorder had turned her inside out; that now her mind was painted on her countenance. Unfortunately all present thought the remark very just.

Another event adds to her disgraces and her misfortunes: her lawsuit came to a trial the day before yesterday, and she was cast by the unanimous opinion of all the judges; costs of suit, damages, and interest.

All in favour of the minors: so that the little she had exclusive of this suit, is all swallowed, and more too by the expences.

As soon as she was informed of this news, although still ill, she set off post in the night alone—Her people say to-day, that not one of them would accompany her; it is imagined she has taken the road to Holland.

This sudden flight raises the general outcry more than all the rest; as she has carried off all her diamonds, which are a very considerable object; and were a part of her husband's succession; her plate, her jewels, in short every thing she could; and has left behind her debts to the amount of 50,000 livres—it is an actual bankruptcy.

The family are to assemble to-morrow to take some measures with the creditors. Although a very distant relation, I have offered to contribute, but I was not at this meeting, being obliged to assist at a more melancholy ceremony. To-morrow my daughter will put on the habit of novice; I hope you will not forget, my dear friend, my only motive in agreeing to this sacrifice, is the silence you keep with me.

M. Danceny quitted Paris about a fortnight ago; it is said he is gone to Malta, to settle: perhaps it would be yet time enough to prevent him? My dear friend, my daughter was very culpable then! You will undoubtedly excuse a mother being difficult in acquiescing to such a dreadful truth.

What a fatality I am involved in for some time past, and has wounded me in my dearest connections! My daughter and my friend.

Who can refrain being struck with horror at the misfortunes one dangerous connection may cause, and how many sorrows and troubles would be avoided by seriously reflecting on this point! Where is the woman who would not fly the first advances of a seducer? What mother would not tremble to see any other but herself speak to her daughter? But those cool reflections never occur until after the event. And one of the most important and generally acknowledged truths, is stifled and useless in the vortex of our absurd manners.

Farewell, my dear and worthy friend! I now feel, our reason, which is inadequate to prevent misfortunes, is still less to administer consolation[1].

Paris, Jan. 14, 17—.

> [1] Particular reasons and considerations, which we shall always think it our duty to respect, oblige us to stop here.
>
> We cannot at this time give the reader neither the continuation of Mademoiselle de Volanges' adventures, nor the sinister events which fulfilled the miseries or ended Madame de Merteuil's Punishment.
>
> We shall be permitted, perhaps, some time or other, to complete this work, but we cannot pledge ourselves to this: even if we could, we should first think ourselves obliged to consult the taste of the public, who have not the same reasons we have to be concerned in this publication.